A DRAGON'S WOLF

THE HIDDEN REALM - BOOK ONE

USA TODAY BESTSELLING AUTHOR
HEATHER RENEE

A Dragon's Wolf, The Hidden Realm, Book One © Copyright 2023 by Heather Renee and HRB Publishing LLC

All rights reserved under the International and Pan-American Copyright Conventions. No parts of this publication may be reproduced, stored in a retrieval system, or transmitted in any form or by any means, electronic, mechanical, photocopying, recording, or otherwise, without the written permission of the author.

This is a work of fiction. Names, characters, places, and incidents either are the product of the author's imagination or are used fictitiously. Any resemblance to actual persons, alive or dead, is purely coincidental.

For more information on reproducing sections of this book or sales of this book, email heatherreneeauthor@yahoo.com.

ISBN: 979-8385883844

Line Editing and Proofing: Jamie from Holmes Edits

Cover: JoY Cover Designs

Illustrations: Art by Kalynne and Samaiya Art

Contents

Dedication

For Jane.
Since you got her daddy...I figured you should have this
one too.
XOXO

MYSTICS

BUCKNER
HALL

CEDAR
HOUSE
COLUMBIA
HOUSE

RAINER
HALL

OLYMPUS
HOUSE
SNAKE
HOUSE

ADAMS
HALL

BAKER
HOUSE
YAKIMA
HOUSE

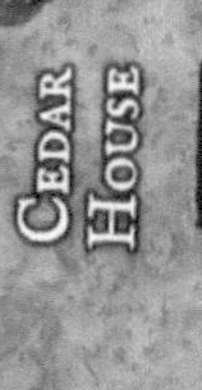

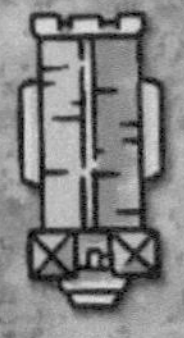

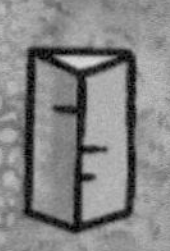

ACADEMY

DragonTail Hall

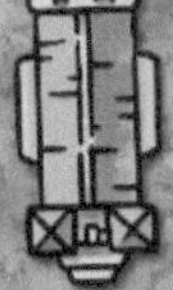
Gym

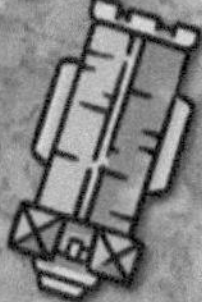
Library

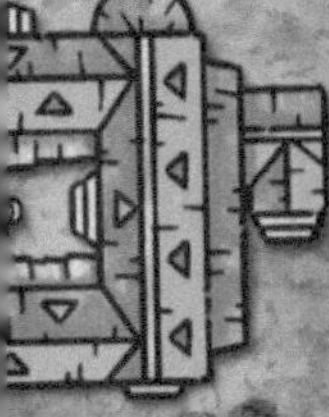

Sparks Cafe

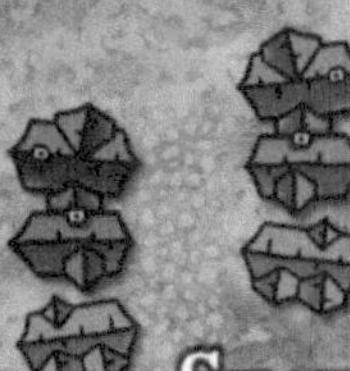
Staff Housing

Chapter One

DAWSYN

One would think that at twenty-two, I'd feel like an adult, but still living with my parents in our wolf pack... Well, that made feeling like anything other than "the alpha's daughter" almost impossible.

Don't get me wrong, I loved my parents and my pack. I even intended to lead them one day—far, far away from now—but that didn't mean I shouldn't want something more out of my life in the meantime.

Our pack had been through some shit. I understood the paranoia that my parents carried over me, but their time for holding me hostage should have expired years ago, and I was finally letting them know that.

"I don't understand why you need to leave," Dad grumbled, crossing his arms and glowering at me with storming blue eyes.

It was a look that frightened our pack members but hadn't made me blink since I was a pup.

My mom—who was thankfully on my side—moved

behind his desk and placed her hand on his shoulder. "Roman, she's already told us that. Three times."

"Don't *Roman* me," he sneered. "*Cait.*"

"I'm just going to go pack and talk to Aunt Sam about which car I can take while the two of you sort the rest of this out," I said, turning on a heel with my hands in my jean pockets, ready to exit my father's office before my leaving the pack grew into an even bigger deal.

"Dawsyn," Dad said, alpha power lacing his words.

I'd thought too soon. It wasn't often that I lost patience with my parents, but even my wolf was done being treated like a child.

She rumbled so loudly in my mind that sound reverberated through my chest. "No." My eyes narrowed at my father as I turned back toward him. He wasn't the only one with alpha power. "I'm leaving the pack. Tomorrow. I tried to do this nicely, but I won't be guilted into staying any longer. You did your job, Dad. I know how to take care of myself. All you have to do is let me prove that."

He and my mother shared an intense look, one I never had deciphered growing up and didn't often mean anything good for me.

"I know," Mom said, switching their telepathic conversation to one I could hear, "but if we force her to stay, we'll lose her in ways we can't come back from."

Dad sighed and ran a hand over his light brunet hair that was only now just starting to show hints of grey, even though he was nearing fifty years old. "She's too much like you."

She smirked and crossed her arms. "And by that, you mean our daughter is capable of many things and that while it's heartbreaking to think about not seeing her every day, she's going to be just fine out in the world without us."

This is why your mother has always been my favorite, my wolf chimed in mentally. *She understands us.*

My wolf wasn't wrong. Mom had spent years telling me about the outside world and making me want to see all the things. She wouldn't have done that if it wasn't what she wanted me to do.

"You said you're going straight to the school to stay with River?" Dad asked, and I knew I finally had him. River was not only my best friend, but the son of my father's oldest friend, Vaughn. My steppingstone to true freedom.

It wasn't as if I would have stayed in the pack even if Dad hadn't agreed with my choice, but not having him upset with me was preferable. Our pack and family were close. I cherished that, and as much as I wished to be my own person—not just the daughter of Roman and Cait Chase—I had no desire to lose the relationship I had with them. Adult or not, they were my family.

"Yes," I answered. "River's roommate moved out. He said I could have the other room and even though it's mid-semester, I can use this time to check out the classes, see what interests me, and get a job."

I'd already thought everything out and, even though I had zero desire to actually go to school, I knew the path of least resistance was leaving first to go to the academy that my parents helped found for young adults like me who wanted something more than the community, pack, coven, or nest life they'd always lived.

"Fine," he said. "You can go and we'll drive you."

I shook my head, my glower returning. "No, Dad. Aunt

Sam already said I could take one of the SUVs. I have the trip mapped out. I know where I'm staying along the way. I know exactly what time I'll arrive based on the number of stops I make. I'm doing this the way *I* planned."

Our eyes locked once more. My wolf rose to the surface, ready to challenge him, but my dad blinked first.

"Okay."

"Okay?" I tilted my head. "Okay, okay?"

He chuckled. "Yes, Dawsyn. Do this your way, but the first sign of trouble and I will be there. And you stick with River. He's been at the school for over a year now. Listen to him."

Of course I would. To a point. While I was older than him, River was my best friend.

I threw my arms around my father and hugged him tight. "Thanks for understanding, Dad."

"I don't know why you're thanking me," he grumbled. "You were going to leave either way."

He knew me so well.

There was no need to rub salt in his fresh wound, so I merely smiled, then hugged my mom next.

Her hold was suffocating, and her body lightly shook. "I'm so proud of you. You're going to have the best time finding yourself and, if you're supposed to, I know you'll find your way back home."

"What?" Dad snapped.

Mom nudged me toward the door of the office. "Go. We'll see you tonight for dinner."

There was a tightness in my chest that I didn't expect to feel after getting their acceptance of my choice. I rubbed my palm over the soreness and let out a shaky breath.

Growing pains aren't just for physical growth, my wolf said, once again reminding me of the old soul I was gifted with.

We'd had our fun over the years, but my wolf was on her fourth lifecycle and sometimes forgot that I was only twenty-two and nowhere near ready to be as old as she was.

My life was only just getting started, and I couldn't fucking wait.

———

FIVE DAYS LATER AND I'D TRAVELED FROM EAST Texas to Southern Washington, about two hours outside of Seattle in the middle of nowhere. Along the way, I'd stopped at several places from the list I'd made, pretending I was a human just for a few days.

Sure, my skin itched and the urge to run as my wolf had nearly consumed me at times, but I had no desire to slack on my adventures, which was how I'd ended up at places like Disneyland, Six Flags, random history museums, and a few other random tourist traps.

I did whatever I wanted, hardly slept since I drove mostly at night, and even though I should have been dead on my feet, as I pulled through the iron gates of Mystics Academy, I'd never felt more alive.

Thick trees with large, full branches and at least thirty feet in height lined the paved, winding road leading to the school. My phone pinged with a message.

River: You're here!

I chuckled. He was such a stalker. Though, I enabled him by allowing him to track me through our favorite app.

Me: *You better be waiting outside.*

A few minutes later, a striking building came into view. It was three stories tall with natural wood siding and steel accents between each of the three floors, along with dark framing around the plethora of windows.

Above the expansive steps, there was a large glass overhang that I parked my car beneath, then searched for River.

The front doors to the main building burst open, and he ran toward my SUV, opening my door before I even had my seatbelt undone.

Before I could say anything, he pulled me into his arms and shoved his nose into my neck, breathing me in. "It's been way too long."

I nodded. Nearly six months had passed since I'd seen my best friend. Between the pack duties I'd been volun-*told* to do and his school schedule, we'd let fall and nearly winter pass without making time for each other.

"Missed you, too," I said with a grin, pushing him back. "Now, quit being such a girl and show me to my new room. I'm exhausted."

He flicked his head back, forcing a few dark auburn strands out of his face, then rolled his hazel eyes, but he couldn't stay annoyed with me for long. He kissed the top of my head, using the six inches in height he had on me to his advantage. "I'm going to regret this."

He made his way to the passenger's seat, and I laughed. "Probably, but you'll love me anyway."

River pointed to the left. "Follow this road until it ends and take a right," he said. "Our building will be second on the left."

I put the SUV into drive and made my way forward. More of the same wood and steel buildings popped up along the road, and there were small groups of supernaturals milling about on the campus. The ache I'd felt in my chest before leaving the pack hadn't actually gone away, and it was back in full force now.

I was actually moving in with River. Thousands of miles from my parents. Holy fuck.

Was I happy? Absolutely. Was I also freaking out? Just a bit.

This was always the plan. River and I had talked about moving together plenty of times when our families got together, but to have it actually come to fruition was something else.

My nerves were a direct result of my parents having kept me mostly confined to the pack all these years. Besides visits to friends that were always done as a family, and resulted in us mostly using portals, I knew nothing of the outside world.

This was completely new for me, but thrilling at the same time, and I was going to embrace whatever freak-out I might have later.

A wolf ran into the road, and I slammed on my brakes. "The shit?" I muttered.

"Yeah, there aren't a lot of cars used around here," River said with a chuckle. "People aren't used to looking both ways."

Clearly. Two more wolves raced across before I proceeded much slower than before. We pulled up to the dorm, and I let out a heavy sigh and squeezed my fingers around the leather steering wheel.

I made it.

River jumped out of his seat and went around to the back, grabbing my bags. I followed to do the same but took a moment to take in the building I'd be calling home for the foreseeable future. It had a glass front with more steel and wood accents like the main building I'd first seen. There was a forest green door and a sign above it that read "Baker House".

I snorted and pointed. "Do you guys bake inside this one?"

River's lips flattened. "No. All the dorms and buildings are named after the mountains and rivers in Washington."

Oddly interesting.

Between the two of us, we carried my couple of boxes and bags inside. I finally grinned, staring up at the three floors of rooms that could be seen from the entry.

I'd done it. Sure, I still wasn't entirely on my own, but who really wanted that?

I was at least out of my pack and with my best friend.

Things could only get better from here.

Chapter Two

CILLIAN

Since arriving at Mystics Academy, three of the five weeks I'd given myself here had already passed. I'd been so certain that I would find the information I needed here. Yet, as I spent hours every day searching the libraries and questioning the eldest faculty as discreetly as I could, I was running out of options.

Not only that, but my patience was wearing thin.

My world was dying, I had to hide who I was here, and the magic around me was suffocating.

Not that Drago had been faring much better as of late. That was why I'd left our realm and come to Earth.

"At the end of this week, we'll have a quiz on shifter history," Professor Dole said, interrupting my thoughts. "So long as everyone passes, then we'll be moving on to shifter magic. Make sure to study this week."

I was barely passing this class, but I wasn't here to earn a degree. Though, I'd at least skimmed the material, so I wouldn't hold the rest of the class back.

The school had this odd rule about everyone learning

and moving forward together. If one student fell behind, the whole class did.

It was odd as fuck.

I left Rainier Hall and headed back to Baker House where my single dorm was. With my head down, I tried to avoid most people, but even more odd than the school's learning practices were the students.

Everyone wanted to know everyone. It was as if they felt entitled to my story, which I wasn't inclined to share. With anyone.

A soft hand gripped my forearms, trying to slow me down, but when that didn't work, they jogged next to me.

"Hey, Cillian," a woman whose name I didn't bother to remember said. Her stride wasn't long enough to keep up with me at a normal pace, but that didn't deter her. "Are you going to the party at Columbia House tonight?"

The question came out breathy, but I wasn't sure if that was more because she was out of shape or something else. Either way, I wasn't interested.

I kept walking. "No."

She huffed and grabbed my arm again, this time using more of her shifter strength. "Are you in a hurry to get somewhere?"

"Yes." I jerked out of her hold with a rumble in my chest that hopefully showed my annoyance.

This time she ran until she was blocking my path on the sidewalk. "Where are you going?"

My eyes darkened and I glared at her, letting my dragon come to the surface just enough to remind her that she wasn't strong enough to stop me—but not enough that she'd know what I really was—and that it would be best if she got the fuck out of my way.

I wasn't at Mystics Academy to make friends...of any sort. I was here to get answers.

She made a small yelping noise, then finally moved to the right. Though, once she no longer had to see my menacing face, she snarled. "I was just trying to be nice because nobody likes you. You don't have to be such a dick."

If only I cared that nobody liked me.

Without turning to look back at her, I continued to Baker House. After that little interaction, I decided I needed to shower.

I stopped at my room on the second floor and dropped off my backpack filled with books I rarely read, then grabbed my towel. Having to share a bathroom with a dozen other guys on this floor was something I still wasn't used to after spending nearly a month here, but that was a small price to pay for answers.

Well, as long as I found what I was looking for by the time I left.

When I stepped out of my room, my nose twitched and chest expanded. My dragon was immediately on alert, but he didn't seem concerned. Instead, he seemed intrigued with whatever we were sensing.

I couldn't use all of my dragon senses without weakening the cloak I had around myself and risking someone noticing me. Normally that wasn't a problem, but given I couldn't speak verbally with my inner beast, I didn't like not being able to tell what suddenly had him paying more attention to our surroundings.

With tenuous steps, I made my way right toward the bathroom. Just five feet from my door, my hands tightened into fists and I sucked in a breath that scorched through my lungs.

Yet, the fire rapidly consuming me wasn't rancid. No, the scent was alluring—possibly the sweetest I'd ever been in the presence of. A mixture of lilacs and sugar.

My brows pinched together. Women weren't allowed in the men's dorms and vice versa. That was a rule that had been in bold and on nearly every page of the student contract I signed.

So, what the fuck was I smelling?

For a moment, I'd thought maybe it was my mate, but that couldn't be right. Maybe this was the magic I'd been looking for. Nannio, my possibly insane or maybe genius grandmother, had convinced me that this was where I would find what we needed to fix the problems within Drago.

As long as this wasn't a mate that I was certain I wouldn't be attracted to, given the previously mentioned rules, I didn't see the harm in investigating the scent that had my mouth salivating and the scales that were buried deep beneath my skin wanting to burst free.

I continued forward, following the sweet aroma. It was coming from the showers. *Fuck.* My stomach churned. I had doubted anyone was practicing magic in the bathroom, which only left my initial thought.

My mate.

A warmth expanded through me, but still, I battled with my thoughts. Something was wrong, and I was going to figure it out, because in my three decades of life, I'd never once...

My inner turmoil was disrupted by singing. A voice so serene that I stopped just outside the bathroom door and closed my eyes.

Thank fuck it was a woman's voice, because I was two seconds from running back to Drago and dying right alongside the realm.

I had two uncles that I loved equally. That just wasn't who I knew *I* was. Fate be damned.

I leaned against the wall and listened to her hum. The longer the soft melody flowed into me, the more I had to fight my dragon for control.

We can't shift here, I reminded him.

The beast inside me wasn't settling, but I was stronger than him most days. I shoved his presence back down and reopened my eyes. Steam was rolling out toward me when I pushed through the door.

The voice stopped, but my movements didn't.

I reached for the curtain, but she peeked out from behind it before I could reveal her body.

"What the fuck do you think you're doing?" Her eyes moved from my raised hand to my confused face.

There was no recognition from her that she knew what I was to her, but seeing her creamy skin, golden eyes, and dark, soapy hair, I knew.

This wolf shifter... She was *mine*.

"Are you mute?" she snapped. "Otherwise, answer the damn question before I give you a reason to be silent."

Maybe she wasn't my mate, because how could she not feel this pull? I could have been wrong, but the need to step closer, even with her just inches in front of me, felt so damn real.

My dragon pushed forward inside me again. I was ready to force him back down, but when the woman before me sucked in a sharp breath, I knew what was wrong.

The cloak around me—the one that made sure the other supernaturals wouldn't realize that I was a dragon shifter—was blocking her from understanding not only *what* I was, but who I was to her.

I forced my dragon down again, then looked her in the eyes. "What are you doing in the men's dorm?"

She scoffed, gripping the curtain tighter between her fingers. "Don't answer a question with a question. It's rude."

"Does it seem like I care?" I replied, matching her attitude. If she didn't know who I was, I wasn't going to show my cards yet. I didn't know her, and I wasn't going to let my realm die just because this wolf shifter was my mate.

Damn it. The lie burned like acid through my mind and all the way down to my stomach. I might have been stubborn, but I wasn't an idiot.

This was my mate. I'd let the whole damn world burn for her.

It didn't matter that I'd only just met her. I knew that truth deep in my soul.

My fingers flinched to reach out and touch her skin, to pull her warmth into me and claim her as mine.

She looked me up and down, still holding the shower curtain like a shield. "Guess not, but then again, you don't *look* like much."

The woman had bite. That was different from what I'd

experienced from the other females at the school thus far. Most of them were like the one who had invited me to the party. Eager for my attention until I insulted them.

Even though it was hard to tear my gaze away from her, this wasn't the place to reveal who I was. She might be my mate, but the supernaturals here didn't understand my kind. Hell, they didn't even remember us. I wouldn't be flippant with my decisions.

With strained effort, I shoved the building desire for this woman down and turned my back on her. "I don't know who you're here with, but you'll get them kicked out if you stay."

Before I could step into my own shower stall as far from her as possible, she laughed and slapped her curtain back closed. "Doubtful, but I appreciate the concern. Asshole."

I pressed my palms against the tile wall once I was alone and took a shaky breath.

Fuck. I didn't even know her name, but the longer I was in her presence, the more certain I became about two things.

This woman was mine, but she was the last thing I was supposed to find here.

Chapter Three

DAWSYN

Normally, I wasn't a complete bitch to people I didn't know. I had no clue what had come over me in the shower, but when I'd sensed something unknown enter the bathroom and saw that guy about to open my shower curtain, I'd lost all sense of rationale.

It didn't help that I was nearly certain he was hiding something. There was a brief moment of recognition that both me and my wolf caught, but it was gone before we could figure out why he could be familiar to us.

Maybe he's been at the pack when you were younger, my wolf offered.

That was a possibility, but doubtful.

Arguing with him had only increased my emotions. Though, they weren't all angry.

The guy was hot as sin with the light scruff on his face, piercing grey eyes, and his tousled umber hair. I may have even been tempted to run my tongue over his body if the situation had been different.

Though I'd managed to keep that thought to myself, it

didn't mean I wasn't feeling the aftereffects of being so close to him.

With hurried movements, I scrubbed at my heated skin and pressed my legs together for any sort of relief to the sudden need I had coursing through me. Finishing my shower and not myself was almost painful, but I managed to get rinsed off and dressed within a couple minutes.

All the while, I forced myself to keep my mouth shut. Though, that didn't mean I hadn't been tempted to say something snarky just to continue arguing with him if for no other reason than to hear his grumbly voice. Thankfully, I managed to stop myself from doing so, but just barely.

He had still pissed me off. Especially when he'd said that I'd get River in trouble for staying in the dorm. I could have told him that I had permission, but immediately using my parents' standing to my advantage went against the very reason I'd left the pack.

I didn't want to be known only as the alpha's daughter.

Even though Grey Eyes—his name until I knew otherwise—didn't know what he was talking about, he'd still made me worry. I didn't want to cause River any problems by staying with him.

As I made my way back to the dorm, I tried to shake all images of the brooding hybrid from my mind, but that was harder to do than I hoped. He smelled of shifters and magic, but the way his chest rumbled made me believe that he did less magic and more shifting.

There seemed to be something foreign in his scent, but that could be just because I'd only met a handful of hybrids over the years.

I waited for my wolf to chime in, but she remained

pensive as I continued down the hallway. When I entered the small space I now called home, I saw River on the couch, legs extended over the carpet as he played some sort of war video game.

"Hey," he said, not even looking away from the TV.

I was still too amped up from the interaction with Grey Eyes, so I went to my door on the left and set my stuff down next to the boxes I'd need to unpack if I didn't want to have wrinkled clothes.

My room was only big enough to squish a single bed against the far wall and a small standup dresser next to it, but it was mine and I loved it. Even if the walls were a dull white and I had nothing to hang up yet.

After letting my hormones settle a bit, I went back to the living room/kitchenette area—they were basically the same space—I sat at the table and faced River, shaking my head as he moved his body and the controller in the direction that he was trying to take the character he was playing.

"Feel better after the shower?" he asked, this time glancing my way.

I shrugged. I'd thought a shower after the long drive would be good for me. If only I'd known that it would be interrupted...

He paused his game and came to sit with me. His hazel eyes stared intently at my face, and then he asked, "What the hell happened in the bathroom?"

"Nothing." I swirled my fingers over the scratches in the light oak wood of the table.

His hand lowered over mine and he tsked. "Dawsyn, do you really think you can lie to me?"

I rolled my eyes and jerked my hand out of his hold as I leaned against the chair back. "It was *nothing*. Some guy just came in there and—"

"Did someone come on to you while you were showering?" His eyes turned to slits, and his voice deepened. Zero to pissed-the-fuck-off in a split second. One of my favorite things about River.

I shook my head. "No. The exact opposite, actually. At least, I think. I don't know. Maybe it's because I'm not around hybrids much, but this guy. He was weird. I couldn't get a good read on him. Like he was hiding something. And he seemed really annoyed about my presence."

"What did he look like?" River asked, calming down only some. This was why my father was okay with me staying here. River was a year younger than me, but he'd acted like the older brother I'd never had for as long as I could remember.

"He had grey eyes, dark brown hair," I answered as blandly as I could while getting up from the table. "Taller. Over six feet. He's a hybrid, but I don't know. Something seemed off about him and not just his shitty attitude."

River grabbed my arm and jerked me back to him, a stupid grin on his face. "You thought he was hot."

"He was a dick," I replied without missing a beat.

"That doesn't mean you didn't find him appealing," he teased, right back to zero with his rage.

I shoved his chest. "Go away, you idiot."

He laughed and took three steps back to the couch, likely to resume playing his games. "There's only one hybrid on this floor. His name is Cillian. You know, in case you wanted to know whose name to be thinking of later on."

Some days I hated River more than I loved him.

Mostly because I really did want to know the stranger's name. Cillian, the hybrid. Not just Grey Eyes.

There were only a million other questions I wanted to ask. Where had he come from? How long had he been at the school? Was River friends with him?

But I didn't. I kept my mouth shut and went back to my room to finish unpacking. I wasn't here to talk about guys or get hung up on one. I was at the academy to spend time with my best friend, see what life was like outside of the pack, and figure out where I wanted to go in a few months once I'd had my fill of River time.

I knew my parents expected me to go back to East Texas once I was done here, but I couldn't shake the feeling that something more was out there waiting for me and my wolf. More importantly, we were only going to find it by being on our own. One day, hopefully not anytime soon.

THE NEXT MORNING, RIVER LEFT FOR ONE OF HIS security classes. He wanted to work under our parents' friends Amersyn and Maciah. The vampires led the groups of supernaturals that provided protection to the communities and hunted down supernaturals who had broken one too many rules.

Given how well he played the big brother role, I was certain it was the perfect fit for him, and I was jealous he so easily knew what he wanted to do with his life.

About an hour after he'd gone to class, I was heading out the door. I double-checked that I had my phone and sent him a text so that he didn't freak out if I wasn't around when he got back later.

Should we head to the forest? my wolf suggested. *Or go see what they have to eat?*

My girl was all about food. I was smart enough to never let myself get too hungry or she was apt to literally bite someone's head off. I learned that once when I was arguing with Aunt Sam.

Food then run? I suggested.

Other way around. Running on a full stomach isn't appealing.

Just don't get hangry and I'm good with that.

She chuckled but didn't respond verbally.

I pulled up the map of the campus on my phone that River had logged into for me. The school had its own app with schedules, live updates from teachers, student contacts, and clearly marked places for us to roam. Handy, even if I wasn't a student.

There were over three thousand acres out here. I eventually wanted to see every bit of the land, but I decided to go easy for our first outing.

According to the map, there was a stretch of land behind the dorms that would lead to a river. I headed that way, seeing students walking in small groups, likely on their way to class, opposite of the direction I was headed.

The school consisted mostly of vampires, wolves, and witches. I'd heard there were a few fae around plus the hybrids, but besides Cillian, I hadn't noticed anyone else.

The sidewalk leading behind the dorms turned to dirt

once the trees came into view. There was a sign before entering the forest that read "All supernaturals are responsible for their own safety beyond this own point".

Well, that just made me feel all warm and fuzzy inside.

There's nobody here who can hurt us, my wolf said.

I'd like to think so, but I wasn't cocky. It didn't matter that I was born from two alphas—one of which was Luna Marked—and that I also carried a strong alpha gene. Training with my mom and aunt had taught me to always assume that the person you were fighting was more powerful than you.

That didn't mean I couldn't win. I just had to be smarter than them, which I almost always was.

Grateful for my shifter magic that kept my clothes safe while I transformed from human to wolf, I pushed my inner animal forward with ease.

My skin tingled and body elongated. Bones broke and moved to new places, and in mere seconds, I was standing on four paws.

We shook our reddish-grey fur out and stretched, a rumble echoing from our chest.

Power filled every inch of our insides. In the next moment, we were running. Since I didn't know the area, I let my wolf take full control. Her senses would get us wherever she wanted to be. I was merely along for the ride. At least today.

Though, that didn't mean I couldn't take control if I needed. Thankfully, we had a mutual respect for each other and that wasn't something I had to threaten often.

She ran through the dense trees, the foliage so thick that the sun above us quickly disappeared and the temperature dropped around us. The ground was still wet with morning dew, and fallen leaves crunched beneath our paws.

Her speed increased, and I could hear the rush of the river getting closer, but then we caught a whiff of something.

Something strong and mouthwatering.

But as quick as the earthy yet sweet—almost vanilla like—scent appeared, it was gone.

What the hell was that? I asked my wolf.

She stopped mid run and searched the area. *Mate.*

I'm sorry. What did you just say?

Our mate, she repeated with even more conviction. *He's here.*

No. No, he couldn't be.

I was supposed to be years from finding him. I had a plan that included not being tied down for the foreseeable future. Not to my parents, my pack, or anyone else. I wasn't anywhere near ready for a mate.

He's gone, my wolf whimpered.

I felt bad for her, but that was possibly the best news she could have given me.

Let's go, I suggested, but not so we could find him. So that we hopefully wouldn't run into him again.

I can hear you, she snarled.

Then, you know how I feel, I replied. *Is it so wrong to not want to know him yet?*

For that, she didn't have an answer. Though, I knew it wasn't because she thought I was right. It was because, if that really was our mate that we scented, there wasn't going to be much in the coming days that we'd agree on.

It was only my second day at Mystics Academy, and I

was oh-for-two on good ones, but I wasn't going to let that ruin this long-awaited adventure.

I was determined to make the best of my newfound freedom. I would find what I was looking for, wolf and potential mate be damned.

Chapter Four

CILLIAN

The southeast section of the forest was almost always empty, which was why it was the spot I frequented when I needed to shift.

I could never do so for long for fear someone would sense my dragon magic, but I also couldn't keep my inner beast pent up for the entirety of my trip.

After checking the area was clear of other supernaturals and making my way to the outermost edge of the academy's territory, I let the shift take over.

Energy slid over me, sending tendrils of magic through my veins. Scales the color of earthy stone with splashes of aqua replaced my light tawny skin, and bones began to break and reshape. With deep breaths, I slowed the transformation to keep the burst of power from exploding too far toward the school.

Refusing that part of the shift lessened the high I normally felt when changing from human to dragon, but it was necessary to keep my dragon safe.

Within a minute, I was on four clawed feet and covered

in scales with spikes along the top side of my neck. Crackles of energy flickered around me, begging to be released. It had been much too long since I'd reveled in my full power, but that was why I had a deadline at Mystics Academy.

I'd need to go home and allow all parts of me to go free, like my lightning energy—a not-so-common ability in dragons that I'd inherited from my father.

I tried not to think about him too often. He'd disappeared into the dark forest when my mother had died from unknown causes. I was only twelve when I'd lost both parents in the same night. My Nannio took me in and raised me with the help of my uncles.

They'd done their best, but the power inside me was tainted with fury at having lost my parents so young. So much so that even I couldn't control myself some days. The closer I got to my five-week cut off, the more my hold was slipping on my true energy.

When I was still a teenager, I'd tried searching for my father, but I stopped trying to seek out the past when I realized that the future was more important.

The future of Drago, to be precise.

According to my uncles, the earthly world wasn't where we belonged. However, if we couldn't keep our realm alive, we were either going to die with it or needed to learn to live with the other supernaturals again, which could be dangerous for us all.

My dragon spread his wings, spanning nearly twenty feet on each side. He flapped them, eager to fly as he was meant to, but that wasn't a possibility for us here.

We'll be home soon, I reminded him, but that didn't seem to help.

His chest rumbled, the only reply I ever really got from him, and he smashed his head into the nearest tree.

Sharp teeth ripped through the bark of the fallen timber, smoke puffed from his mouth, and white lightning flickered around us, causing small fires in the leaf-covered ground that my dragon at least stomped out with his feet.

When we didn't have to hide who we were, I considered our movements one, but with so much pressure to remain hidden, I didn't let myself completely merge with the animal inside. It was causing my chest to feel heavier by the passing days, but I needed information on magic more than I needed to bond with my dragon.

He paused, sucking in a strangled breath, and we both listened for sounds.

Fuck. We weren't alone any longer.

Normally, I tried to let him run between the trees or lounge in the water for at least half an hour, but it seemed as if our time was going to be cut short today.

We need to shift back, I demanded, but he wasn't listening to me.

His head swiveled to look north, and his front claws dug into the earth.

No, I snarled loudly.

He merely growled in reply. A proper dragon "fuck you" to me.

Finally, I caught the scent that was distracting him.

Damn it. This was exactly what I didn't need this morning. It was Dawsyn. At least, I assumed that was her name since I heard the other residents of Baker House talking about the woman staying with River when I left earlier.

Shift. Now. My voice was deep and released more dragon magic than I should have, but it was the only way to make him listen with our mate so close.

His wings flapped and head thrashed around for several more seconds, but he finally relented.

Painfully, thanks to his lack of agreement, I was back on two feet, fully clothed.

I'm sorry, I said to him. *We'll come out here again soon. Or maybe we'll even go home.*

Based on the hollowness suddenly filling my chest, that last bit didn't make him feel better.

It was time to go back to the school and find the answers I so desperately needed so that I could figure out what to do about Dawsyn.

I might have wanted to claim her the moment I saw her, but we didn't always get what we wanted. A life growing up without my parents and feeling like an outcast had taught me that lesson many times over in my thirty years.

AFTER ANOTHER FAILED LIBRARY VISIT AND THE earlier shift cut short, my mood was worse than it had ever been. My mind was distracted with thoughts of Dawsyn and how best to keep distance between us, but also with the pressure to figure out how to save my realm.

Neither task seemed doable at the moment, but I was determined not to fail. Whether that was at both or just the latter remained to be seen.

With my head down and hands shoved in my jean pockets, I stormed through the halls of the main school building where the faculty offices were. People moved out of my way without me having to slow or say a word.

I should have been more cautious of how much power I was exuding to make that happen, but I needed five minutes of not giving a damn.

By the time I reached the exit, I wasn't any better off. I shoved the doors open, almost hitting another student in the face.

"Dude, what the hell?" he snapped, but I didn't bother looking up.

I merely growled and heard his feet move faster in the opposite direction.

And this was why nobody liked me here.

Good thing I didn't care.

As I rounded the corner to get back to the dorm, a small body slammed right into me. I sucked in a breath, ready to unleash the full force of my rage on the idiot stumbling over me, but then *her* scent consumed me.

The smell of lilacs and the sweetest sugar filled my lungs, spreading through the rest of my body. All the fury I'd been holding on to dissipated.

Shit, this wasn't good.

When it came to Dawsyn, I'd been trying to settle on indifference until I could attempt to uncomplicate the situation. Now, it didn't seem like fate was going to give me the time to do so.

"Cillian," she seethed.

Clearly, she hadn't gotten over our first meeting, but maybe this could play in my favor. If she continued to hate me, I wouldn't be inclined to fuck everything up for my realm by telling her who I really was.

"I'm flattered," I said hauntingly. "You asked around about me enough to figure out my name."

Her sneer deepened. "Only because I was complaining about you to River."

Yep. She was the one the others were talking about earlier. I couldn't remember if I'd ever seen her roommate before, let alone talked to him. Though, that didn't mean a part of me wasn't jealous.

Aggression started to build up inside me again, thinking about her staying with another man, but I tamped it down. Barely. "Would that be the idiot you're going to get kicked out for letting you stay in the men's dorm?"

She laughed in my face, staring me down without an ounce of fear. "Sorry to disappoint you, but River won't be getting in trouble for me living in Baker House."

I bent down to her height, a mistake I realized too late because being lower meant getting closer to the mouth I suddenly wanted—no, desperately needed to claim.

"How do you figure?" I forced myself to ask.

Her nostrils flared and cheeks flashed crimson. "I just do."

Maybe it was time for me to do my own research on this particular shifter.

No, I chastised myself. This was exactly what I didn't need. Something—or someone—that was going to distract me from my purpose here.

Fuck. It was as if I was being torn in half. Finding a mate in Drago was a precious and rare thing. I knew that and I didn't want to dismiss her, but if I didn't, I put so much else at risk.

Instead of continuing this conversation, I strode past her, bumping her shoulder in my haste.

She whirled around and wrapped her fingers around my wrist. "Don't fucking brush by me as if I'm beneath you."

Before I turned around, a smirk lifted on my lips. Touchy. I found it endearing and probably shouldn't have.

I swiveled back to her and first stared where her touch was currently branding my skin. I shook her off with feigned annoyance, then leaned in closer, our noses barely an inch apart. "You *are* beneath me. For more reasons than you could ever imagine."

As the harsh words fell from my mouth, it was as if a knife was being thrust deeper and deeper into my heart. I'd just made my choice, even if I didn't agree with it and my insides felt as if they were burning to ash.

I was choosing my realm over my mate.

What the fuck was wrong with me? It was a question I didn't have an answer to and probably wouldn't anytime soon. My only hope was that I could come back and apologize later, but I couldn't be what she deserved if I didn't fix my realm first.

I couldn't bring my home back to life if I screwed up now, but I might be able to salvage our bond.

Even knowing that, every syllable spoken to her physically caused me pain, starting in my chest and expanding through the rest of my body until it felt like my blood was fire.

With every bit of strength I contained, I walked away from her, surprised when she let me have the final word. A little disappointed even.

But this was for the best. For the time being, anyway.

I had an entire realm and race of supernaturals to save. Getting distracted with a mate, who—if history remained true—wouldn't understand who I was, wasn't in the cards for me.

No matter how much I might have briefly hoped otherwise.

Chapter Five

DAWSYN

It was as if the universe was taking sides and proving my parents right. Between the failed run in the woods where we scented a possible mate and the proceeding interaction with Cillian, I was ready to tuck tail and go back to my pack.

I'd expected the academy to be... Well, I wasn't sure what exactly, and maybe because I was staying in a men's dorm, I thought I'd feel more welcomed. Maybe thinking I knew what I was walking into was where I'd gone wrong.

Out of all the times we'd visited the other packs, the covens, and nests—hell, even Fae Islands—nobody had ever treated me the way Cillian had. There had been respect, friendliness, and I wasn't sure how to describe it, but I'd never been made to feel as if I was "less than" when I'd traveled to other places until now.

Worse, the infuriation thrumming through my veins had hints of attraction weaving through.

Attraction I wanted nothing to do with. Especially knowing that a mate could be somewhere around here and that same scent I'd caught earlier was not wafting off the brooding hybrid.

I wanted to be grateful for that, but I was having a hard time ignoring the disappointment that seeped into me. The attraction I'd felt toward him even when we were arguing was fucking powerful. Knee-weakening and pulse-pounding. It didn't matter that when he spoke, I wanted to cut his tongue out. My body still yearned to be closer to him.

Gah! What the hell was wrong with me?

I didn't know and didn't have time to psychoanalyze myself. I was joining River for dinner where I'd be meeting some of the friends he'd made since arriving at Mystics Academy. I kept my fingers crossed during the rest of my walk, hoping they would be more pleasant than the shitface I'd just left behind.

The small building called Sparks Café came into view, and I nearly choked on my own breath. The exterior was made of white stucco that glittered wherever the sun reached. Even worse, there was a man's sparkling face painted on the glass doors. A man with brunette hair, a smirk, and black sunglasses on. One that looked eerily similar to a particular human-created vampire...

I hesitantly opened the door, and things only got worse —or was it better—from there.

I thought Twi-hards had died out after all these years. It had been four or five decades since those books and movies had come out. I knew that, because my mother used to love them. You know, before she realized she was a wolf shifter.

That was also why I recognized the interior theme of the café. It was an exact replica of the one from the movies.

Ones that I'd been forced to watch when I was younger with my mom and Aunt Embry. Though, I couldn't deny that listening to Aunt Embry poke fun at the fake supernaturals for hours on end merely to annoy Mom had been more than entertaining.

River stood from a table in the back right corner, waving at me. "Over here, D."

I joined him, two wolf shifters, and a vampire, then waved awkwardly as everyone watched me. "Guys, this is Dawsyn," River said, wrapping an arm around me and using his other hand to point at his friends. "That's Justine, Craig, and Parker."

Justine was a vampire with two rows of perfect teeth. She smiled at me, showing them off, along with her muddy-red eyes, ebony hair, and skin like snow. It wasn't often that I met young vampires since they couldn't have kids, but she looked maybe eighteen. The thought of someone turning her that young made my stomach churn, but I didn't relay my thoughts on the matter.

"I've been dying to meet you ever since River told us you were coming," she said. "Being the only girl in this group is painful most days."

Her grimace made me laugh as I sat next to River in the offered chair. "Glad I can help shift the tides."

Craig, the wolf shifter in the middle, scoffed. "You're one of us. You're not supposed to take her side." His dirty-blond hair fell over his light-green eyes as he stared me down.

"Sorry to disappoint, but I left my pack behind for a reason," I said with a wink. "I was on Team Justine before I even walked through the door."

She raised her hand and held it over the table. Mine quickly smacked hers. Parker, the last guy, groaned. "I told you to keep your mouth shut. You've just made everything so much worse."

He was on the smaller side, possibly not even six feet, which was a rarity for a wolf shifter. His dark-blue eyes seemed friendly enough, though. Not cocky, but someone who knew he was smart and didn't have to brag about it.

He reached a hand toward me. "Nice to meet you, Dawsyn."

I shook it and returned his crooked grin. "You, too."

Craig groaned and shoved Parker. "Don't play the nice guy to win her over. River said no touching."

I raised a brow at my best friend. "Did you cock block me before I even arrived?"

Several things happened at once. River covered his face with both hands. Justine laughed so hard she spewed water on everyone, and I was pretty sure Craig's and Parker's hearts stopped beating for several seconds.

"I should have left you in the dorm," River complained, wiping water droplets off his arms.

I grimaced. "I don't even want to go back there."

This had all eyes returning to me.

"You can stay with me," Justine said eagerly. "My dorm doesn't have the same stench that River's does."

As nice as that sounded, I wasn't running away from this particular problem. Though, I wasn't willing to admit why. At least, not at the moment.

"Thanks for the offer, but I can handle an annoying hybrid for the short time I plan on being here," I said, reaching for my own drink.

I didn't get the chance to grasp the glass before my best friend grabbed my arm.

"Did Cillian say something else to you?" he asked with unmasked annoyance.

I shook him off. "It wasn't anything I couldn't deal with on my own."

Only I didn't really *deal with* anything. The asshole had gotten the last word, because by the time I'd thought of a decent comeback, he was already ten feet away. I'd known immediately that it was better to ignore him than come off as slow.

River didn't seem to want to let it go, though. "Seriously, Dawsyn. What happened?"

Once again, everyone was staring at me, and I wasn't pleased with my best friend for putting me on the spot.

"Drop it, River," I snapped. "I took care of it."

He at least let go of me. "Fine. We'll talk about it later. Just stay away from him."

"Not that I intend to purposely throw myself in that hybrid's path, but I left my pack so people would stop dictating what I did," I said lightly. "You won't be doing the same. Best friend or not."

Justine mercifully broke the tension when she threw a fry at River's face. "Yeah, don't be a twat, Riv."

Craig and Parker laughed, River cracked a smile, and I just shook my head, trying to enjoy the moment, but I couldn't shake the thought of wondering if I'd made a mistake.

I'd expected to fit right in. To feel at home with others at the academy. Yet, a part of me felt more lost than ever.

I should have had a plan B. That thought disappointed

me more than I was prepared for. I'd been so certain this was the path that I needed to take to find what I was looking for, but the churning of my stomach and the weirdness with my wolf... Something wasn't right.

I should have thought of a backup plan months ago. Instead, I'd stayed singularly focused on hanging out with River and getting away from the pack.

Well, more specifically, no longer being labeled the alpha's daughter.

The expectation to participate in all the pack things, to lead, to be...perfect. It had been too much for too long. This was supposed to be my break. Yet, I felt even more unhinged than I ever had back home.

Maybe the predictable life I'd been living hadn't been as bad as I'd made it out to be, but I wasn't ready to throw in the towel on the hopes I had when setting out on this path.

I just wanted to be me. An imperfect wolf shifter who enjoyed her alone time, but also wanted to be with a group of people, being one of their peers. Not someone they'd one day call their alpha.

"Can I get you something to eat, hun?" an older witch approached and asked, disrupting my thoughts. She wore jeans and a surprisingly clean white blouse. A pencil was stuck in the short grey hair just above her ear, and she held a pad of paper between her hands.

"Sure," I said, expecting her to reach for the pencil, but she never did. "I'll take a double bacon cheeseburger, fries plus onion rings, a large chocolate milkshake with whipped cream, and what kind of pie do you have?"

She looked back at the counter and squinted. "Apple, peach, and cherry."

"A big slice of apple, please," I added, then noticed every food item I'd rattled off was being magically written on the paper in her hand.

"You got it, hun." She glanced around the table. "Anything else for you birds?"

My brows pinched together and I realized Justine, Craig, and Parker were staring at me with slacked jaws.

"What?" I asked.

"Did you order all that for just you?" Justine still gaped at me.

I glanced at River who was hiding a smile behind his hand. "Was I not supposed to?" I asked, but he didn't respond first.

Justine gave me a once over and shook her head. "You maybe weigh a hundred and twenty pounds. Where does it all go?"

"Oh." I guessed River hid his *healthy* appetite from his friends. That wasn't going to be me. "Shifter blood. Our metabolisms burn through energy quickly."

Justine sighed and slumped back against her chair. "I miss enjoying food that much."

I wanted to use that as my opening to ask about her being turned, but doing so within ten minutes of meeting her probably wasn't proper new-friend etiquette.

"River eats the same, usually," I said. "I've seen it myself. Bottomless pit over here. I would have assumed the same about Craig and Parker."

My best friend rolled his eyes at me. "We try to be polite in front of Justine. Unlike some people."

There was a loud thump under the table, followed by a groan from River. My eyes looked at Justine, who was glaring hard at him. "Don't be stupid." Then, she reached over and smacked the backs of Craig's and Parker's heads as they snickered. "That includes all of you idiots."

Craig crossed his arms and lowered his eyes, mumbling on about how River just *had* to invite his friend to come stay here.

There wasn't a chance in hell I was going to apologize for being myself in front of the vampire. Even if she was newly turned and still adjusting to her blood diet, pretending I was someone that I wasn't wouldn't help her.

Though, instead of feeling proud of myself for not hiding who I was, I found my thoughts going back to Cillian and wondering if he, too, was pretending to be someone he wasn't.

RIVER HAD NIGHT CLASSES A FEW EVENINGS A week, and after our dinner together was one of them. Justine offered to let me hang out at her place, but I declined. I needed time to decide if I was going to let my attraction to a grumpy hybrid screw with my plans or if I was going to figure out all the things this place had to offer.

Besides sexy men and people-pleasing supernaturals.

I grabbed my phone and called the one person I knew I could trust to give me advice that wasn't biased—even if she was my mother.

"Hey, Sweetheart," Mom's voice sang through the phone. "How are you?"

I grinned even though she couldn't see me. "I'm good. How is everything with the pack?"

She chuckled. "You've barely called since leaving—much to your father's dismay. Do you really want to talk about the pack?"

Mom never was one for small talk.

"It seemed like a good opening."

"Oh, Dawsyn." She sighed. "What's going on?"

I had no desire to tell her I felt like maybe I'd made a mistake, but something in my heart was conflicted, and I knew there was no way I was going to work out the truth from my subconscious without telling her everything. Even the stuff I might have been wrong about.

Once I started rattling off everything that had happened for the last couple days, I couldn't stop. I told her about the shower incident, my run, and how I scented something odd. Though, I wasn't ready to tell anyone that my wolf was certain our mate had been close.

Then, I went on about running into Cillian again today and the interesting dinner with River and his friends.

"None of it is what I expected," I said as I finished rambling.

"I'm going to say something you probably don't want to hear, but given you called me, I'm also certain you want the truth," Mom said, and she wasn't wrong. "You've lived in the same place for twenty-two years. A place where what's been expected of you has always been clear and somewhere that hasn't really changed during your lifetime. You've also spent several years dreaming of leaving the pack and experiencing the world, but up until now, you've only seen things as the alpha's daughter."

"I don't understand what you're getting at," I said when she paused.

I could hear the smile in her voice as she continued. "What I'm saying is that while you've visited other packs, covens, nests, and communities, you've done so as a special guest. We've been treated with a certain...respect after everything your father and I have been through. That respect has been passed on to you. Until now. Am I safe to assume you haven't told anyone you're getting special treatment staying with River because of who your father is?"

Of course I hadn't. I didn't want to be the alpha's daughter, much less one of the school's founders' daughters.

"Your silence confirms my assumption," Mom said, "but there's nothing wrong with that. You just need to change your perception of the situation."

"How am I supposed to do that?" I asked, leaning back on my bed and closing my eyes.

"First, trust yourself and your wolf," she answered. "You left home for a reason. You might not know what that reason truly is, and that might scare you, but letting go of the fear is the first step to finding what you're looking for. Trust that you're in the right place at the right time."

A grin formed on my face. "Is this my mother speaking or the Luna Marked wolf?"

"Maybe a little of both." She laughed softly, then turned serious. "Something about this hybrid calls to you."

A statement. Not a question. I wanted to tell her no, especially since I'd possibly scented my mate, but I still didn't want to tell her about that.

"He's different," I replied.

"I was once different, too. That's not always a bad thing."

No, I didn't think it was, and I had nothing against hybrids. This one was just an asshole to me when I'd never given him any reason to be...while making me want to lick him from head to toe.

"Thanks, Mom," I said. "I love you, but I need to go. Tell Dad I said I love him, too, and I'll call you guys again soon."

"Love you too, Sweetheart."

I stayed laying on my bed long after the call ended, but even with my mom's advice, I wasn't seeing anything clearer.

Chapter Six

CILLIAN

Part of me hadn't wanted to leave my room the next day. I didn't want to chance seeing Dawsyn again. The bond I could feel expanding inside me was growing stronger, causing the drive to search her out to be at the forefront of my thoughts.

Only, she didn't know who I was, and I needed to keep it that way.

I'd tried mind-linking my uncle and Nannio, but neither of them replied to the nudges I'd sent. Just another thing that had my agitation growing.

Given my shittier-than-normal mood, I decided to skip my morning class and go to the library. It was a massive five-story building with books donated from packs, covens, nests, and even the fae. The first three floors had already proved useless to me.

There weren't any books about sourcing spells or charms, the very thing I'd been focusing on since my arrival to Earth.

Something was sucking the life out of my realm, and

until we could find the source with a spell, there wasn't a damned thing anyone seemed to be able to do about it. Not even the eldest dragons knew what was happening, and given our world had never had an elected leader, just a chosen few who led meetings, it seemed as if nothing was getting done.

Uncle Jerome was one of those "chosen few." He was good at keeping the shifters happy, but he wasn't the best at sussing out information. That was something I normally helped him with, but I felt like I was failing now.

I made my way to the fourth floor. A guy was just coming down the stairs when I turned the corner to go up. He had thick, black-rimmed glasses on and was wearing wrinkled khakis with a blue polo that had some sort of food stain right at the center of his chest.

He was a hybrid with low levels of magic radiating from him, nothing that made me think he could be useful. At least not to me.

I continued past him without another thought. On the fourth floor, I started out at the front left corner and intended to zigzag my way around to the other side. Each previous section had taken me a week to get through, but I was running out of time. If I had to ignore all my classes to look through these books in just a few days, then that was what I'd do.

The teachers had mostly become dead ends anyway. Except for Professor Hayes. He was harder to get alone than the others and I wasn't giving up on him.

My fingers moved over the aged spines—some torn, some pristine, some made of cloth and others of leather. It seemed that the further up in the library I went, the older most of the books became.

They covered wars, origination of the supernatural races, spell books, the history of the previous supernatural council, and everything else in between. I focused mainly on the spell books, flipping through each one that I came across in hopes I'd find something that could work for my realm.

Dragons couldn't do magic like witches could, but our scales held a certain power that other supernaturals didn't understand. We couldn't create new magic, but the energy in our scales allowed us to replicate certain things.

For one, a cloaking spell like I was using while on Earth. It wasn't foolproof. I couldn't convince another supernatural that I was human, but I could muddle my energy enough that I at least passed as one of the new hybrid children being born around the world.

If I could locate the source spell and figure out the ingredients needed, then there was a chance I could use the power in my scales to activate the incantation.

Sure, we could have asked a witch for help to make it easier, but telling anyone that our realm existed was a mistake we only made once, nearly two centuries ago.

Most thought the stories of dragons flying over the Earth were fable, but at one point, we all worked together. At least, until one too many of the other races decided that harvesting our scales to increase their own power was better than having us as allies, according to the history books back in Drago.

I'd grabbed a few origin books over the past few weeks, but there wasn't anything about my kind in them. Uncle

Jerome had told me when I was young that they'd forced a witch to erase dragons from the memories of everyone. As I got older, I didn't think that was quite possible. There had to be some sort of record written down somewhere.

That somewhere wasn't within the first three floors of this library, A library that was supposed to be the biggest in supernatural history. Another reason why I'd come to the school in the first place.

I moved quickly through the books, finding less and less witch-related ones as I went. By the time I made it to the back left corner, I heard footsteps coming closer.

My intent was to ignore whoever was up here, but that only lasted a split second before hints of sugary sweet lilacs invaded me.

Damn it. Why was this female everywhere I was?

My dragon rumbled inside my chest, and it wasn't hard to imagine what he was thinking.

Fate was pushing my mate to me.

With my nose in a book, I silently hoped that she would see me and go away. Only that didn't happen.

"What the hell are you doing here?" she demanded, standing at the end of the aisle I was in.

Slowly, I lifted my eyes from the pages they weren't actually focused on. "Studying." I deadpanned.

Her hand raised, and she pointed at the book I was holding. "Witchcraft from the fifteen hundreds, huh? What class is that for?"

"If you're so interested, why don't you go see one of the counselors so you can enroll in some yourself?" I asked, looking back toward the book.

Keeping my eyes on her creamy skin, golden eyes, and

long, dark caramel hair wasn't helping me to keep my resolve around her.

She stomped toward me and poked a finger at my chest. Words left from her mouth, but I didn't hear a thing she said as I fought with my inner beast to stay contained.

Scales threatened to poke through my skin, and my chest heaved as I squeezed my eyes shut. Fuck. She needed to leave.

"Are you even listening to me?" she snarled.

I hoped my silence would make her walk away, but that was quickly dashed when the palm of her hand slammed into my shoulder.

"You arrogant, son of a...." Her words trailed off, but her hold on my shoulder increased.

The tips of her fingers pressed into my shirt, and she sucked in a sharp breath.

I tried my damnedest to hold back, to keep the cloaking shield in place, but her touch was too much. She'd shattered the spell with the heat of her hand and the power of our bond. There was nothing I could do but finally look back up at her.

My eyes opened, and she was staring slack-jawed at me. Her golden eyes practically glowed in the dim light of the library, and she seemed almost frozen in place besides the rapid rise and fall of her chest.

"You're not a hybrid," she whispered.

Not exactly what I expected to come out first, but we could start there.

The bond between us was wrapping around my chest, demanding I touch her like she was doing to me, but I managed to stay where I was as I confirmed her statement, silently demanding my shield to go back up.

"No, I'm not."

She licked her lips and tilted her head. "You're something else. I feel like I should know what, but I don't."

"Because you're not supposed to." The words came out harsher than I intended them to, breaking whatever stupor she'd been in.

Her open palm curled into a fist, and she punched me in the chest. A literal spark of magic ignited between us, but instead of that drawing her closer, she moved back several steps.

"What the fuck are you?" she asked with disdain.

My mouth opened to lie to her, but acid rose up my throat, making me pause.

"You can't just..." Her hands waved in front me. "Be all that and still not talk to me." Then, her eyes locked with mine, the glow around them grew brighter and a rumble echoed from her chest. "Tell me who and *what* you are. Now."

Heavy energy laced her words, pressing down on me. The desire to tell her everything was right there, but I managed to hold my tongue long enough for me to get the shield over my dragon energy again.

"I'm a dragon shifter," I admitted quietly. Even though I couldn't sense anyone else up here, that didn't mean I shouldn't be careful.

She blinked several times, then spoke again like before. "Where did you come from?"

Tendrils of power seeped into my skin, and I growled. "What are you doing to me?"

The smirk on her round face did nothing to help my demeanor. "Alpha power. It's not only helpful with my pack."

"*Your* pack?" I asked, setting the book I'd been checking out back on the shelf.

This woman couldn't be an alpha. She was young, maybe early twenties, and not the least bit intimidating.

Her arms crossed over her chest. "Yes, *my* pack. The one I will inherit one day if I so choose, but even if I don't, I'm still an alpha and you'll show me some damn respect."

She was even sexier when she was angry with her lip curled up like it was then.

"And if I don't?" I taunted, moving in until I practically stood over her. "What are you going to do?"

She attempted to shove me away, but I was prepared for that and kept my feet planted right where they were.

"You're an asshole," she muttered with a heavy sigh.

I chuckled darkly. "Tell me something I don't know."

She looked up at me, eyes softer yet determined. My chest caved in on itself as I waited for her to say whatever had flipped her mood from furious to something else that I didn't understand.

"You're my mate, but that's not the part you don't know," she said confidently.

I cocked my head to the side, leaning casually against the bookshelf even though my heart was racing. "Enlighten me then."

She stood straighter and didn't give a moment of hesitation before she said, "I don't want a mate."

Well, fuck.

Chapter Seven

DAWSYN

ate was a cruel bitch with a sick sense of humor. How could Cillian be the mate I'd scented in the forest? How could the one person who'd been an utter asshole to me since I arrived be the one that I was supposed to spend the rest of my life with?

I didn't know, and honestly, I didn't want to know. He seemed surprised by that.

Kind of like how I was still in shock over knowing he was a mother-freaking dragon shifter.

The creases around his eyes smoothed out a few seconds after I'd said I didn't want a mate, and he straightened. "You didn't say you didn't want me."

Oh, this cocky prick.

"I don't want you," I corrected. Though, my stomach churned while I said the words, and I was pretty sure if I opened my mouth again too soon that I was going to throw up on his boots.

My body wanted him badly. Traitorous bitch.

Cillian leaned forward. "I smell bullshit."

I was hoping to hurt his pride enough that he'd agree with me that this whole mate business was a terrible thing, but I wasn't sure I was going to get what I wanted.

Is rejecting him really what you want? my wolf interjected. I hesitated in my response, giving her the ammunition she was likely looking for. *You don't know what you want.*

Maybe I didn't know everything, but I was certain that I didn't leave my pack just to be tied down a mere week after getting my freedom.

"You can smell whatever you want, Cillian," I said. "But the proof comes from our actions. I haven't thrown myself at you, and I think that says a lot about what I think and want. Or better, don't want."

His eyes traveled over my face, then down my chest before glancing briefly toward my feet and coming back up. "You don't have to throw yourself at me to want me. Foreplay comes in all forms."

"You sound like you're talking from firsthand experience," I countered.

His hand moved to rest on the shelf above my head. "Tell me, Dawsyn. Why are you here? Right now, in this library?"

I rose onto my toes, refusing to let him intimidate me with his height or energy. Though, now that I was thinking about that... I couldn't sense the unique shifter power that I did before.

"This is a public space," I said. "I have every right to be here, and there was no way for me to know that you were lurking in the shadows, reading shit that has nothing to do with you. Maybe you should tell me why a dragon shifter that shouldn't even exist wants to learn about witches from the 1500s?"

That had him flinching. Good. This asshole couldn't act all high and mighty when his mere existence was questionable as shit.

"You have no idea what you're talking about," he seethed, backing up a step.

At least I could breathe a little easier.

"Then, feel free to enlighten me," I replied. "Otherwise, I might need to go asking about some things to other people who won't piss me off as much as you do."

He lurched forward faster than I could react. His hands wrapped softly around my arms, and he leaned forward until our eyes were level. "You can't tell anyone about me." His words were pleading, and the fear pulsing off him that my wolf was picking up on made me briefly find some sympathy for him.

Very briefly.

"Then, you better tell me what the hell you're doing here," I said, remaining strong.

Even if he was the victim in whatever situation he'd found himself in, I wasn't going to pretend I didn't just meet a damn dragon shifter. Though, as much as I thought I'd be freaking about this revelation, I also remembered why I was coming up here in the first place.

My mother was Luna Marked. She was born human, to very human parents. Yet, she turned out to be one of the most powerful wolves in the supernatural communities.

I'd asked her about her past more times than I could remember over the years, and she'd always answered me, but there was something deep down that niggled at me.

Did her fate change mine? Did I need to be worried about her Luna Marked blood running through my veins?

According to my parents, they couldn't find any information on past Luna Marked having children, and the Moon Goddess Luna hadn't reappeared to them since I was born. Unless we found something in old text, or she came to us, there was no way to know.

I didn't like the unknown.

Cillian's hands were still on me, but he'd yet to start talking. I raised a brow at him while ignoring the delicious heat radiating from him that my skin was lapping up like an excited puppy. "Either you start talking, or I start walking."

I could hardly breathe from his touch, but my words had at least come out strong.

Cillian seemed to still be conflicted over what to do, but I didn't have time for that.

My body jerked back, breaking the hold he had on me, and I turned to leave. Games weren't my thing, so I wasn't going to put up with his, no matter what, or who, he was.

"See ya, asshole." I waved my hand in the air even though I couldn't see him, but I didn't even make it to the end of the aisle before my back was being pressed against a shelf.

Cillian boxed me in with both of his arms. His eyes darkened, and his stare switched from my lips to my glare several times before he finally spoke. "You can't leave."

"If you don't want your balls in your throat, courtesy of my right knee, then you better back the fuck up," I said calmly, even though my hands were shaking at my sides.

He leaned back with his upper body, but he didn't remove his arms from blocking me in. "I'll tell you what you want to know, but only if you make a blood promise not to tell anyone else. Not your family or best friend. Nobody can know about me."

On one hand, I was perfectly okay with that. I didn't want anyone to know I'd found a mate I didn't actually want, but on the other hand, how the hell was I supposed to sort out that dragon shifters were alive and well—at least this one—if I couldn't talk to someone about this?

You can sort it out with your mate, my wolf said.

He's not ours, I replied. *We don't know where he came from or why he's here, and I don't want any part of whatever shitstorm it seems like he's in with all his secrets.*

But he's our mate. How can you say that?

Pretty freaking easily, actually, I said. *You of all people should know that.*

She didn't immediately respond, so I gave Cillian my full attention again. "What the hell is a blood promise?"

He tilted his head to the left. "Seriously?"

I rolled my eyes. "No, I just enjoy asking stupid questions."

"You're...difficult." His lips thinned. "A blood promise is an unbreakable vow. We share a drop of blood with each other, and the words exchanged between us can't be shared unless we both agree."

"Yeah, no. Not happening," I spat out quickly. I wasn't going to be sharing anything with this man. Plus, a third option had finally come to me. "I'm going to go now, and you're going to let me. If you don't, my wolf is going to rip your throat out. I don't care who you are or what you want. I'm done with this craziness."

I slipped out from under his arm and took only one step forward before my wolf spoke up again.

I've been mated to his dragon before.

I paused mid-step. *Come again?*

His dragon spirit. I've been with him before. You can't leave him, Dawsyn. He needs us.

What in the shittery shit was I supposed to do with that information?

"What's wrong?" Cillian asked from much too close behind me.

"Nothing you need to be concerned with," I said without turning back toward him. "Can you just accept my verbal promise not to tell anyone for now? Trust that I'm not a heartless bitch and won't out you unless I have no other choice?"

He stayed silent for several beats. If he didn't agree, I wasn't sure what my next play would be, but my heart couldn't continue to ignore my wolf's wants, no matter how much my mind preferred to.

"Okay," he said a minute later.

I peeked over my shoulder. "Okay?"

"Yes, I'll choose to trust you," he said, then added, "For now."

That was good enough for me. For now.

Chapter Eight

CILLIAN

Throughout my entire life, I'd never needed to verbally speak with my dragon more than I did while standing in the library with Dawsyn. He was thrashing around inside me when Dawsyn started to walk away, only calming when she paused.

I didn't think we could trust her, but after thirty years communicating using only emotions with my inner animal, it wasn't hard to decipher that he didn't agree with me. Hell, he more than didn't agree with me.

My dragon wanted Dawsyn. More than he'd ever wanted anything before.

Yet, I had no fucking clue why.

While I'd told Dawsyn I would trust her, my intent was to still hold back information. She seemed hellbent on ignoring the mate bond, and that made her dangerous to me. If my dragon forced me to lower my guard with her, she could easily destroy us. I wasn't going to let that happen. No matter how he felt.

If I was being completely honest, it was no matter how

I felt as well. I could want Dawsyn all I wanted, but if she didn't return the feelings, that changed everything.

"Do you have specific questions you want answered?" I asked once we retreated further into the corner of the library. "Or should I just start talking?"

"Where did you come from and how come I can't sense your dragon energy anymore?" she asked, her eyes looking me over with trepidation.

"I was born and have lived in Drago all my life," I said before she cut me off.

"What is Drago?"

I leaned casually against the wall. "I would have gotten there next if you hadn't interrupted me."

She stayed silent this time, briefly glancing behind me at the window to our left.

"Drago is another realm outside of Earth," I answered. "Much like where the fae live."

Her brow creased. "But that's on Earth."

"No, the entry point is on Earth," I said. "The islands themselves aren't part of this world. They're in another dimension of sorts. Like Drago."

"Do you access *dray-go*"—she sounded out the word slowly—"from Earth like the islands?"

This was one secret I wasn't willing to share. "Only supernaturals with dragon energy can find Drago."

I wasn't technically lying. A spell had been cast to make it so that nobody else could enter our world, but that could easily be removed for us to operate exactly like Fae Islands. Only, I didn't foresee that ever happening.

The mountain out in the middle of the Beartooth

Range of Montana would forever remain hidden if my people had their way.

"How are you blocking your energy from me?" she repeated her earlier question.

"It's just part of my abilities," I said. "Like shifting."

My teeth ground together from the lie. Apparently, the bond was intent on punishing me if I chose not to tell my mate the truth. Except telling her that my scales held magical properties when she'd just said she didn't want me as her mate seemed like a poor choice on my part.

"What are you doing here?" she asked next, watching me more closely than before and making me wonder if she somehow knew I hadn't told the truth just a moment ago.

"I'm trying to find something for my world," I answered.

"What?"

Of course she wouldn't just let that answer be.

"I don't know exactly." That wasn't actually a lie. "But I believe it's a spell and I figure when I stumble upon it, I'll know."

She crossed her arms, her eyes full of suspicion. "Why you?"

"Why not?" I quipped.

Her fingers drummed over her forearms. "You're not telling me everything I want to know."

"Maybe not," I replied, "but I'm telling you everything you need to know and a hell of a lot more than I should."

Our stares locked in a battle of wills. When I first met her, I didn't sense the alpha power she easily wielded on me earlier, but I now knew not to underestimate her. I just hoped she wasn't as stubborn as she was strong.

"Fine," she relented. "Are there more of you here, hiding among the other supernaturals?"

My head shook. "At least, not that I'm aware of."

It was possible other shifters had slipped out of the realm over the years, but not likely. Our energy was often much "louder" than the other races. Someone would have outed any lingering dragons years ago since it wasn't until recently that we could blend as a hybrid.

"Do you need help with whatever your problem is?" she asked, tone sincere and breathing even.

Color me shocked. I didn't expect that.

At least, not the sincerity of it.

"No, I can handle this on my own," I answered, but the words caused my chest to rumble again even though I hadn't thought they were a lie. Maybe deep down I had. That was a consideration for later.

She licked her lips and brushed her caramel hair behind her shoulders. "I don't have any other questions right now, but that doesn't mean we're done here."

I finally grinned again, side-eyeing her. "Given the larger forces at play, I didn't assume that would be the case."

Her huff in reply was almost appealing. "My opinion hasn't changed. I don't want a mate."

There was no way she wasn't feeling the same pull I was. Even if she'd been coming to the library for her own reasons, fate had still led her to this particular part of the building. To me.

"I've never heard of unrequited mates," I said. "Do you assume pure will is going to keep us from each other?"

"Will. Desire to be alone. Alpha strength. Disgust. Whatever you want to give credit, go for it," she said, her words flippant, but with my enhanced hearing, I could hear the racing of her heart. She wasn't as sure about staying away from me as she wanted to be.

My first thought was to agree with her. A mate bond couldn't be more powerful than ourselves. If neither of us wanted the other, there should be some way to prevent anything from coming to fruition.

Except...

The dragon spirit inside me was strong. His wants weren't always easily ignored, and based on the continued storm brewing inside my chest, he wanted this wolf. Badly.

It didn't matter that she'd essentially just told us we weren't good enough for her. The need and want and lust for this woman growing inside me was almost too much to ignore, and those feelings only grew each time I touched her.

"I guess we'll just see what happens," I replied.

She glanced behind us, then back at me. "How long are you here for?"

"Why? You worried I'll leave without saying goodbye?" I winked for good measure, but the curling of her upper lip cut my confidence down more than I wanted to admit.

"Just wondering if I need to worry about you throwing off the balance of energy here," she said. "You might be able to conceal your dragon power, but that doesn't mean it's not present."

Her voice was full of authority and showed me that she took her innate alpha position seriously. Even if it seemed as if she'd run from the responsibility. I had a feeling that becoming an alpha when gifted the inner power wasn't something one couldn't just ignore. Much like a fated mate bond.

"I assure you, my energy isn't going to be a problem," I said. "Once I find what I'm looking for—which should be soon—I'll be gone and you won't have to *worry* about me or my dragon energy."

Saying those words made my throat burn and my stomach twist, but they were what needed to be said. At least, for now.

The rest I'd have to figure out later. In fact, maybe it was time for me to go home and check on things there.

If my family wasn't going to answer my attempts at contact, I would talk with them face-to-face.

Dawsyn would probably even appreciate the reprieve.

Well, as long as the bond didn't push her to follow me... That was a situation neither of us were prepared for and could possibly get her killed.

Chapter Nine

DAWSYN

Walking away from the library was...uncomfortable. For many reasons. Not only because of everything I'd just learned, but because the bond—the one I thought I could avoid if I just didn't sense my mate again—was thrumming like a live wire inside me.

I wanted to cut it off from my heart, because Cillian made one thing clear without having to say the words that I hadn't been afraid to say.

He didn't want a mate either.

At least a part of him didn't.

The stupid part, my wolf snarled.

She wasn't happy, and after her earlier admission of having been mated to his dragon spirit in the past, I didn't blame her. Just because I'd stayed to hear him out, though, didn't mean I'd changed my mind. A part of me still believed that we didn't need them, that we were better off alone. Except, the more she opened herself up to me, the more I knew getting her on the same page as me wasn't going to be easy.

While challenging my wolf was sometimes a favorite pastime of mine, we were still one. Making sure she was happy was just as important as doing what was best for me.

Even after the last hour of revelations, I still thought it was best for us to walk away from Cillian, but I wasn't completely shutting down the idea of something far in the distance happening with him.

I'd heard the stories of my parents' failed rejection. My mother hadn't wanted my father in the beginning. Apparently, I was more like her than I realized, a fact that frightened parts of me for more reasons than I cared to recount.

Though she'd eventually figured things out, I wasn't sure my choice would be as simple.

Why? My wolf asked. *Because you're just as stubborn as she is.*

Possibly more, I joked, but she didn't find that as funny as I did. *All I'm saying is that both Cillian and I seem to have a lot going on internally. I want to experience the world on my own, and he has his realm to deal with. Plus, do you expect me to keep this secret forever and just disappear on my blood family and pack? You know we can't do that.*

We also can't abandon our mate when he so clearly needs help.

I groaned aloud while walking down the sidewalk. I didn't want to agree with her, but my heart was the most trusted part of me, and the pulsing there as she said those final words told me, deep down, that I agreed with her.

Being supernatural came with more benefits than most people often knew what to do with, but it also meant that we often had little control over the direction of our life.

Fate was demanding like that.

I needed to talk this out. When I first promised Cillian that I wouldn't tell anyone about him being a dragon shifter, not some shady-ass hybrid, I didn't actually think I would keep my word.

Except now, the thought of telling River or anyone else instantly made bile churn in my stomach.

Mother-freaking mate bond.

This was going to be a major pain in my ass.

"Hey, Dawsyn," a friendly voice called out from behind me.

I turned to find Justine waving enthusiastically at me and smiling, showing off her pointed fangs.

Thankful for the distraction from my screwed-up situation, I waved back and waited for her to catch up.

Her hand drifted under her nose and she chuckled. "Your wolf has a particular scent. You were easy to find."

"Uhh, I'm not sure how I should take that," I said, hoping I wasn't going to have to punch one of River's friends right in her face.

"Definitely in a good way," she replied with a grin. "You're an alpha, yeah?" I nodded. "Thought so. It's not always easy to tell with you shifters, but something about you... I don't know, but I'm sure glad you're here."

Her continued cryptic words weren't making me feel any better, especially when I'd just been trying to find information about the possibility of me being more different than I was prepared for.

"Why are you glad I'm here?" I asked as we kept walking in the direction I had been. Though, I wasn't sure where I was going. Heading back to the dorm and potentially having to lie to River about Cillian didn't sit well with me, especially after my best friend had made it clear last night that I should stay away from the not-hybrid.

The vampire looped her arm through mine and turned us toward the main building, but instead of going to the front doors, we stayed on the sidewalk that curved around the side toward the back. "I'm not just *glad* for your presence. I'm ecstatic, because being the only girl in our group of friends isn't always the best. They might eat like dumbasses, but outside of that, it's like they have no shame. Burping and farting are usually a staple during our hangouts. With you there yesterday, I didn't once have to block my sense of smell. I swear, it's like they forgot they were supposed to be adults now."

My pity instantly rose for her. I had thought River grew out of that kind of childish behavior, but according to Mom and Aunt Embry, men never really did learn to "grow up."

"I can put the fear of alpha power in them as often as you'd like me to," I said with a smirk that continued to grow. "That sounds really fun, actually."

It could be something to distract me from this mess with Cillian. For a short time, at least.

"That would make my year," Justine said with glee. "How do you feel about coffee?"

I looked her dead in the eyes. "How do you feel about living?"

She let out a sigh of relief. "Thank the Gods. The last girl I tried to be friends with hated coffee. I didn't know how to get past that flaw."

I chuckled. While I enjoyed my caffeine doses, I didn't

love them *that* much. Though, I was good with encouraging the vampire's obsession.

"Where's the best place to get coffee around here?" I asked. "I've only been making it in my room."

She shuddered. "I'm so sorry. You've been truly deprived."

My head shook, but my smile grew. It seemed as if the vampire loved her coffee more than she did the blood she needed to survive.

"We're going straight to Cappa's Cart," she said, increasing the speed of our previously leisurely walk.

Once we got to the backside of the main building, a large section opened up, looking a lot like a city park with benches and trees for shade and even a few water fountains. People roamed around in small groups and sat out under the sun, either in the grass or on the benches with books spread around them. Though, it still wasn't warm out, so I didn't quite understand the appeal of lounging around.

Some of the groups were loud, a lot of them quiet, but best of all, none of them paid us any attention. Not that I normally stood out in a crowd, but after learning that Cillian was my mate, it felt as if there was a red "A" on my chest. Like everyone would know what had happened and there was nothing I could do to control the situation.

Fear was just as much of a fickle bitch as fate.

"Here we are," Justine announced with a blissful sigh. "Cappa's Cart. The best coffee in the world."

A tall and stocky man blushed from behind the six-foot-wide silver cart. "You just say that because you like the extras I put in your drink."

She rested her arms over the counter and grinned.

"Come on, Bruno. You know me better than that now. Would I come here three times a day for mediocre sustenance?"

He shrugged, his dark hair moving lightly over his shoulders. "Maybe."

"Now, for the goods," she said with a waggle of her perfectly arched brows. "I'll have my usual, the Vampy Triple. My friend here, Dawsyn, she's new to Mystics Academy. Let's give her Caramel Trouble with your special sprinkles."

Bruno winked at me with his friendly, chestnut eyes. "Can she handle the sprinkles so soon?"

I winked right back at the dark-skinned barista. "There's nothing I can't handle, Warlock."

He leaned slightly forward and laughed deeply, holding his stomach. "Oh, you're going to be fun."

Justine wrapped an arm around me. "I bit her first."

"Easy, Vamp," he said, beginning to make our drinks. "You have nothing to worry about with me. Now, Cillian on the other hand..."

My eyes widened, and I sucked in a breath so hard that I started to choke.

"Cillian?" Justine asked with raised brows. "I thought he was an unsocial asshole?"

After a few more coughs, I finally said, "He is." Then, I turned to Bruno. "Why the hell did you say that?"

His voice lowered, and he set Justine's concoction in front of her but kept his eyes on me. "My cart is like the local watering hole. I hear all. Like how you were seen going up to the fourth floor of the library just a short time after Cillian and both left minutes apart."

"That, like, literally just happened." What the hell was wrong with people that they found my whereabouts *that* interesting?

He shrugged, working on my coffee. "News travels fast around here, but don't worry. They were more worried about your safety than anything else."

Well, that was...good, I guessed.

Though, it also confirmed that my paranoia wasn't unfounded earlier, worried that I was walking around and drawing unwanted attention to myself.

Justine took a long pull of her hot drink. "Perfection as usual, Bruno."

Crimson stained his russet skin as he handed me my cup. "You're too kind."

A knowledgeable, yet self-conscious warlock barista. That was one hell of a combination.

I lifted the drink to my lips, but Justine smacked my forearm before I could take my first sip. "You have to inhale first. Use all your senses to enjoy this kind of delicacy."

Yeah, she definitely loved her coffee *too* much.

Though, I indulged her and took a whiff over the steaming lid. Caramel, dark-roasted beans, sweet, heavy cream, and even a bit of cinnamon hit me first. There were other, lighter scents that I couldn't quite make out over the stronger ones, but put all together, I couldn't deny that my mouth was watering.

"You're a coffee connoisseur, Bruno," I said and raised my cup to him. "Thank you."

He bowed, another flush appearing on his cheeks. "I hope I'll see you again."

That was a given. Though, it wouldn't be as often as I suspected he saw Justine.

Once we paid for our drinks and said our goodbyes, Justine led me out the back left of the common area, which was what the grassy area was apparently referred to as.

"Are you going to take any classes while you're here?" she asked me as we passed by one of the class halls on our left, this one called Buckner Hall.

To our right was more forest area. Instead of answering her, I caught myself wondering if that would be a better place to run with my wolf than the one we'd been in previously.

Justine poked me hard enough that, if I didn't have accelerated healing, I would have expected a bruise. "I didn't peg you for a daydreamer," she said inquisitively.

I shrugged, sipping my coffee again. "I'm not normally. It's just been a weird few days."

"Would Cillian have anything to do with that?" she asked with a waggle of her brows.

Yeah, I wasn't having this conversation with someone I just met.

"Not really," I answered, doing my best to keep my breathing even and pulse steady so she wouldn't sense the lies I was spewing. "Sure, he was a jerk the few times I've run into him, but he doesn't concern me."

"Uh huh," was her only reply.

She absolutely didn't believe me. I didn't take offense, though. I wouldn't have, either, but I'd at least tried to cover my ass...or was it his ass?

And in her defense, she at least didn't push the subject.

"You're from Texas, right?" she asked.

I nodded. "Born and raised. What about you?"

"New York," she answered. "All these woods took some getting used to when I first got here last year." Then, she nodded toward our left. "I'm right here in Cedar House. You want to come in?"

"I need to get back to my dorm for a call I'm expecting, but next time?"

Her face lit up with joy. "I'll hold you to it."

This was the part I had been looking forward to by getting out in the world. I never imagined I'd befriend a vampire from New York, but I liked Justine already.

My only aversion was having to lie to her about Cillian. Having to lie to anyone about the dragon shifter wasn't sitting well with me, and that was the real reason I was heading back to my room.

I had some shit to sort out. Being alone was the only way to do that.

Chapter Ten

CILLIAN

Going back to Drago after telling Dawsyn who I was didn't seem like the best choice, considering she was my mate. Being away from her didn't sit well with me. Except the next morning, I woke up in a cold sweat. Something was wrong, and it had nothing to do with the feisty wolf shifter.

I didn't know what was going on, and my uncle and grandmother still weren't answering my attempts at mind-linking. That pissed me the fuck off.

It was an eight-hour drive to the mountain entry point located in Montana. Not something I wanted to do, but I needed an update on my world before I could continue my search.

Or figure out what the hell to do about Dawsyn.

She'd been on my mind all night, and I'd slept like shit knowing she was so close, yet untouchable.

Our closeness in the library had screwed with my head, and my dragon's persistent rumblings weren't helping.

Now that I was in my truck, headed east and increasing the miles between us, the thought of her only intensified.

The bond between us was far from being solidified, but apparently that made no difference in the amount of discomfort I felt while driving away from her. If I didn't know better, I'd have sworn there was a knife slowly being pushed through my heart. The harsh breathing coming from my lungs and the nausea settling in my gut were making things worse.

All this and I'd only been on the road for three hours.

Turning up the music on the radio, I tried to drown out my thoughts and aches with mindless tunes. Thanks to the shitty station choices I had while in the middle of nowhere, though, it only served to give me a headache.

Cillian? my grandmother's voice echoed through my mind.

Nannio, I growled in return.

Boy, do I need to remind you what respect for your elders means?

Do I need to remind you *that it's rude to ignore your grandson when he's in a different realm?*

She huffed. *It couldn't be avoided. Things have… escalated around here and not in a fun way.*

What's wrong? I demanded, pulling the truck over so I could fully focus on our conversation.

I could hear pans banging in the background. *Are you cooking?*

That didn't bode well for anyone. Nannio hated cooking and only did so when she wanted to poison someone.

None of your business, she retorted. *Where are you right now?*

Halfway between the academy and the entry point home.

Why in all the dragon eggs are you there? Another strong huff. *Seriously, boy. I told you not to leave the school.*

And I asked you to keep me updated. Do you remember the last time we talked? Her silence was answer enough. *Over a week, Nannio. You can't keep me in the dark that long if you expect me to stay here when I can't even get a hold of Uncle Jerome.*

It would have been helpful if I could have gotten in touch with anyone else in our clan, but mind-linking only worked with blood family.

Something happened, didn't it? she asked. *Did someone figure out who you are? Damn it. Can you seduce them into silence?*

I snorted and hit my fist against the steering wheel. *Doubtful.*

How did this happen? Never mind. It doesn't matter. Threaten them if you need to, Cillian. We are in a war here, and it's not going to get any better without you finding that spell.

What the hell is going on now?

Things were tense when I'd left, but people still went about their daily lives. I'd known my mission was important, but I didn't think it was urgent. Why else would my grandmother have insisted I enroll in classes I didn't really need?

Listen carefully, Cillian, she said, lowering her voice. *More importantly, first promise me that you'll turn around and go back to Mystics Academy?*

Not fucking happening.

I'm going to whoop your ass when I see you for using such language toward me, she reprimanded. *Now, promise your Nannio before I come there myself.*

Damn it. She absolutely would do something as stupid as that. My grandmother was pushing two centuries old. She couldn't hold her magic like I could. Her being on Earth would create waves none of us had time for.

I promise to stay here, I said begrudgingly. *Now, stop avoiding my question.*

Do you remember the lightning flashes we were seeing on occasion?

Of course. Mostly because I'd been accused of causing the disruption.

When I was in my dragon form, I could call lightning to me. It took a lot of effort and concentration, but I'd honed my skills over the last few years. Though, I only ever used it far away from the main town. The new lightning we'd seen was striking closer and closer to the main buildings each time it appeared.

Two buildings have been destroyed and it's not just lightning anymore, Nannio said. *It's balls of white fire as well.*

Why the hell didn't you tell me sooner? I shouted through our connection.

Because this isn't your problem, she snapped back. *You are where you're supposed to be. I sent you to Earth for a reason. Now, find a solution to our problem like you're supposed to and sort your shit out with whoever knows about you. Only then can you come back home.*

It sounded as if she'd banished me. I almost called her

out on that, but decided I didn't need to put the idea in her head for future use. She wasn't one of the leaders, but my grandmother was a force to be reckoned with.

People didn't often tell her no unless they had a death wish.

I'm doing my best, I finally replied.

Do better, she said, but softer this time. *I need to go. Next time don't be such a baby if you don't hear from me. If everything goes to shit, you're better off where you are, anyway.*

Nannio, I snarled, but she'd already cut the connection.

Stubborn old lady. I was going to...do nothing about this once I made it home, but more importantly, my motivation for finding the spell Drago needed had just increased.

I needed to get back to the academy and talk to my mate.

Too many hours later, I was back at the school and had parked my truck in the small garage the academy had next to the faculty housing. I ran back to the dorm, and instead of dropping the bag I'd packed back in my room, I went straight to Dawsyn's.

Only I'd forgotten one thing.

She didn't live alone.

River answered and pushed me back before stepping into the hallway and closing the door behind him. "What the hell do you want?"

The wolf shifter had always been quiet around me. He

never paid much attention to me, but always seemed to be aware of my presence. I'd thought of him as a weaker wolf, but maybe I'd been wrong to make that assumption.

"I need to speak with Dawsyn," I said, holding the strap of my bag tighter at my side.

"No." He crossed his arms and widened his stance.

My eyes roamed over him with a raised brow. "No?"

"Yeah, man," he replied. "I don't give a shit who you are or how badass you think you are. Nobody gets to be a dick to Dawsyn and keep showing up without consequence."

I wanted to laugh in his face, but at the same time, my mate having someone who was willing to protect her like this... I couldn't be angry about that.

Though, that didn't mean I wasn't going to keep playing the role I'd begun to perfect since arriving here.

I took a step closer. "Are you going to be delivering said consequence?"

He didn't flinch or back up. "I'm not afraid to, but I'd rather you just left her the hell alone."

That spoke volumes. Fighting between supernaturals was cause for immediate expulsion from the school. I knew River was here getting certified to be one of the supernatural guards. If he was willing to give that up for Dawsyn, maybe I didn't have to be such a dick.

"Good to know," I said, then relaxed my stance. "Where is Dawsyn?"

"I told you, you're not getting to her," he replied.

Treading carefully wasn't usually my strong suit, but River was an obstacle I couldn't just move through or disregard.

"I heard you," I said. "I'm just making sure she's good.

Last time I saw her, she didn't look like she felt all that well."

It was a lie that I'd only just come up with, but didn't seem to surprise River, making me assume Dawsyn actually didn't feel okay.

"Interesting." River's eyes peered closely at me. "Well, she's inside and sleeping and you need to go."

"I assume you won't be telling her that I stopped by?" I asked for pure amusement.

He chuckled and grinned at me. "Abso-fucking-lutely not."

When he opened the door and slipped back in, I tried to get a look inside, but my eyes never spotted what they so desperately seeked.

My dragon was at least happier being back at the academy. Knowing Dawsyn was safe in her dorm was good enough for both of us.

I, however, wouldn't be resting anytime soon.

If I wasn't going to have Dawsyn's help, then I needed to resort to persuasion. Or seduction, as Nannio called it.

One way or another, I was going to find that spell and help my realm. That had to come first. Otherwise, I was going to have nothing to offer Dawsyn as a mate.

Even if she wanted to accept the bond, I needed to focus on Drago. Without my realm, I'd be nothing more than the last dragon in existence and powerless without my connection to the clan. I'd be a weakness for her, which wasn't a future I was willing to accept.

Chapter Eleven

DAWSYN

Death was an awful feeling. I had no idea what was wrong with me, but the day after learning Cillian was my potential mate, I started losing my mind.

My wolf wasn't really speaking to me. There was a pounding in my head that was only eased by sleep, and the ache in my chest never ceased. It only pulsed with a steady thrum that eventually made my hands shake.

I'd considered telling River the truth of everything that had been happening in my delirium, but I managed to keep everything to myself, including the worst of my aches and pains. If he'd known how shitty I was truly feeling, he would have called my family out of concern. There wasn't a chance in hell that I wanted them here.

Failure wasn't an option. I wasn't going to go back to my pack with my tail tucked between my legs. Whatever this was, I would figure it out. I had to.

River's head peeked into the room. "How are you doing today?"

"Better, but groggy," I answered. "What time is it? Hell, what day is it?"

He chuckled and came over to my bed, sitting next to my prone form. "It's six p.m. on Friday."

I groaned and kept my head on the pillow. "I can't believe I've been in bed for two days and still feel exhausted."

Yeah, that was a lie. I was still laying there, because I knew if I got up that the floor was going to feel like it would drop out from under me.

"Neither can I," he said. "More importantly, I'm not letting you sit in this room any longer. I know something more is up with you besides being overly tired, but maybe this is all because you're not doing *anything*. You need people. You belong to a pack, and socialization is part of that."

My head lifted a bit. "Tell me more, Dr. River."

He gave me a half smile and ran his hand over his mussed auburn hair. "I think you're homesick." I opened my mouth to reject the claim, but he placed his palm over my face. "Let me finish. Yes, I think you're homesick, but I don't think you need to leave. You just need to find a way to make Mystics Academy home. At least, temporarily. You've never not known what you were going to do, and now you're floundering. Words that are said with all the love I have always had for you."

If only he knew how much I was truly *floundering*.

I'd yet to mention Cillian again and neither had River. I hated lying to him by omission, but even though I didn't want the dragon shifter as my mate, I still felt obligated to keep his secret. Just another reason I subconsciously hadn't left the dorm.

Running into Cillian again didn't seem like the best idea.

He would make you feel better, my wolf said.

How the hell do you know?

Because he's our mate. You're fighting the connection, and this is the consequence to that.

Fate is making me hurt because I don't agree with them? I baffled. *Well, fuck that.*

If there was one thing I hated most, it was people trying to control others. Fate still constituted as people in my book.

I wouldn't be forced to love someone. Not now or ever. Not even if I was being punished for my refusal.

The annoying part was that I'd been attracted to Cillian before finding out he was my mate. Now, just so I could make a point, I felt as if I *had* to reject him. Or at least figure out how to prolong accepting the connection between us.

It wasn't as if I was repulsed by him. I could see a future between us, but only once he sorted his shit out and I'd gotten to experience life without my choices being dictated by someone else. Plus, if I jumped all-in with him now, where would that leave me?

Going back to his realm that wasn't faring well and possibly getting myself killed? Never seeing my family again or being able to explain to them what was going on?

River tapped my forehead. "Is anyone home?"

"Yeah, sorry." I pushed myself up until I was sitting next

to him. "What do you have in mind for my needed socialization?"

His grin grew three times its normal size. "Well, there's this party…"

My groan returned. "You know how I feel about parties."

"I know, I know. They're just a reason for people to drink, spew their real feelings, and then pretend they don't have any recollection of said spewing, but the parties here are different. There's very little alcohol since nobody wants to get expelled for breaking school rules and, just like you've already experienced, everyone is chill. There are no expectations."

Not everyone was chill, but I understood his point. "Will Justine be there?"

"Are you trying to replace me?" His lower lip jutted out, and I shoved him back.

"Of course not, but you'll know lots of people there," I said. "If you want to go off and talk to someone that I don't, I want to know I have someone else to hang out with."

"Alright." He let out an exaggerated sigh. "But I'm still your number one."

I got up and patted his shoulder. "Always. Now, hold my hand and walk me to the bathroom so I don't fall down thanks to my legs getting hardly any use lately."

His responding chuckle lit up something within my chest that had felt dead the last couple of days. Maybe my best friend was right. I just needed to get out of this room and stop being afraid of running into Cillian.

I'd come to Mystics Academy to find out who I was on

my own. Finding him first didn't mean my priorities had to change.

His presence wouldn't control my decisions any more than I intended to let fate do so.

It was time to go out and live my life, just how I'd been hoping to.

Surrounded by new friends, from different races and places around the world, who could remind me that there was more to this life than being the alpha's daughter. Or someone's mate.

Two hours later, I'd tried to eat some bread only to throw it up. I then drank water only for it to make my stomach churn ten times worse. I'd finally tossed my hands into the air and forced River to get me out of the damn dorm.

Only he wasn't as sure about his idea anymore. "You haven't been honest with me. There's something actually wrong with you, isn't there?"

I straightened my shoulders and forced a smile to my pallor face. "I'm fine. I just need some fresh air. You said this party is in the west forest, right?" He nodded. "Maybe I'll even shift and go for a little run. I'm overdue."

Yes, we are, my wolf grumbled.

It's not my fault I've felt like shit.

She made a harumph sound and I rolled my eyes. My wolf was just as stubborn as I was.

"If you're sure..." River said, his hand reaching for the door.

"Absolutely. Lead the way, beastie."

He threw his head back and laughed loudly. "I haven't heard you call me that in years."

I returned his smile easily. "I know. I'm thinking we need to bring it back. Even if it's only to give us a good laugh."

His arm slung around my shoulders, and he guided us out of the dorm. "You got it, *beastie*."

The light tone of his voice offered me some normalcy, but as soon as we were out in the hallway, the tension in my chest increased. My body instinctively wanted to go left, telling me that was the direction of Cillian's dorm, but River was taking us right, toward the stairs and the exit.

Stupid mate bond.

I waited for my wolf to snark at me with something, but she remained quiet. I liked that even less than I liked her insistence that Cillian was the answer to our problems.

When we exited the building, there were a few groups ahead of us, walking in the same direction. "Are all the students invited?" I asked, shivering from the cool winter temperatures. Supernaturals ran hot, but even thirty-degree weather got to us. My long-sleeved sweater, jeans, and knee-high boots weren't keeping me as warm as I'd hoped.

He nodded to my question. "There's a student bulletin where things like this are posted. You'd have access to it if you'd enroll in at least one class."

"You know I'm not here to learn about the things they teach in the classrooms," I reminded him. I was there to learn from the people. Make new friends that weren't directly attached to my parents. To forge my own path in this world.

"But there are classes that go over all the things you want to do," he replied.

My head shook and I lowered my voice. "No, those are classes for people too shy to make new friends on their own. I think that's great for them, but that's not a problem I have."

Half of the school had been built for trade degrees like River was taking to become one of the guards, and the other half was for those who maybe didn't come from great communities or had lost their families over the years and were searching for something else.

Yes, I was searching for something else, but I didn't believe that a class was going to give me what I wanted.

"Says the person who spent the last several days holed up in her room." He scoffed, then added. "What are you going to do when the new semester rolls 'round and your parents get pissed you're not taking classes?"

"I'm a grown-ass adult," I reminded him. "I wanted my father's permission to leave the pack, yes, but he doesn't get to dictate when I come home."

River tsked at me. "But he can kick you out of my dorm."

"Well, I'm going to get a job," I said. "When the time comes, I'll rent a place nearby, or maybe the dean will grow fond of me and let me stay, regardless of what my father wants."

He barked out a laugh so loud, the sound almost made me jump. "Yeah, because Dean Fuller is the kind of man to say no to Alpha Roman Chase. Keep dreaming, D."

River was right, but that didn't mean my plans needed to change. The start to my adventure had been rocky, but I was determined to make the best of this. I would find my place here. If I couldn't, maybe I'd travel to LA to spend time with Aunt Andie. Hell, I could even go see Aunt Lucy on Fae Islands. She was always game to piss people off.

Though, that wasn't my end game here. I just wanted to figure out who I was as Dawsyn Chase. Not Roman and Cait's daughter. Not someone's mate. Just me. Standing on my own two feet.

Actually, now that the thought was there, Aunt Lucy might be the perfect person to talk to.

"How are you feeling?" River asked me as we approached the tree line.

I took a deep inhale and tilted my head to the side. "Better. I told you, I was just tired. Hell, maybe even you were a little right, *beastie*."

His hazel eyes appraised my face, then wandered down the rest of my body with his mouth turned down. "Are you sure?"

I shook my arms out at my side, rose up and down on my toes, and a rumble escaped from my chest. "Yep. Everything is working as it should. I still have a headache, but it's not throbbing like earlier. A little fresh air was all I needed."

Not my mate or anyone else, I added silently to myself and my wolf.

River stayed at my side, not moving any closer to the party we could finally hear and see.

I grabbed his hand and tugged him forward. "Come on. I'm freezing and that bonfire looks like a dream right now. Plus, I see Justine. If you don't want to go with me, I'll ditch you for her."

He snarled. "Yeah, you're feeling better. The threats are back. Just what I've been missing in my life this week."

My arm looped through his, and I leaned my head on his shoulder. "You know you love me and my threats."

"Unfortunately so," he grumbled while fighting a grin. "Even on the days I wish I didn't. But ride or die, I've got your back, D. Just stick with me."

That I could do.

Chapter Twelve

CILLIAN

I'd officially lost my mind. After River had refused to let me see Dawsyn, I had two options. I could plow through him and do whatever I wanted, or I could be patient.

Patience was fucking brutal.

My classes had been forgotten about, and I was barely keeping my dragon in. The longer I was apart from Dawsyn, the more certain I was that I was going insane.

The need to just lay eyes on her was making my skin crawl and chest ache with a ferocity I hadn't felt since my mother died and my father disappeared nearly twenty years ago.

I'd lost both parents in the same day, and now, it felt as if I was losing Dawsyn, but in reality, I knew she wasn't mine to lose.

The wolf shifter had made it very clear that she didn't want a mate, but I couldn't be the only one feeling this frantic. How could she fight this and stay locked up in her room?

That question had led to many moments when I wondered if River was the one keeping her from me, but if he knew I was Dawsyn's mate, something told me I would have heard from him already.

I was laying on my dorm floor, fighting the need to shift, when I finally heard Dawsyn's voice out in the hallway and caught her scent.

My door had been left cracked open with only the chain lock keeping it from opening to just anyone. While the extra noise hadn't been helping my mood, it had finally paid off.

Dawsyn was leaving her room.

I undid the chain lock and my eyes landed on right where she stood. Only she wasn't alone. River was with her. She looked terrible, but there was a smile on her face. One that I knew would disappear the moment she saw me.

With strained effort, I closed my door and changed out of the clothes I'd been wearing for the last two days, and then headed out. By this time, Dawsyn and River were already outside and walking toward the forest.

They weren't the only ones, either. There must have been a party going on. Though, "party" seemed like a terrible name for it. I'd checked out some of the events around the academy, hoping to find a loose-lipped teacher who would tell me something useful.

Only there was rarely ever any alcohol involved, and people seemed to just stand around a fire or the tables of food talking to each other. Occasionally, there was dancing, but that did nothing for me.

Getting physically close to any of the residents within

Mystics Academy had been the furthest thought from my mind.

Until Dawsyn showed up.

I followed them from a distance and noticed that the longer Dawsyn walked, the taller she stood. Her shoulders were no longer hunched, and she held her head up like I was used to seeing.

I couldn't see her face long enough to see if the color was back, but I assumed it was. I wanted to think that was because she was near me, but she had no idea I was close. My scent was cloaked for a reason.

I was tempted to go up to her, but something told me that would only trigger her and River. Normally, I didn't give a fuck about pissing people off, but I'd heard enough over the last week to understand how close those two were.

Dawsyn would choose River over me without blinking an eye, which meant I needed to be patient. I'd been learning a little too much about patience lately.

If all I could do during the party was watch her from afar, then that would have to be good enough. At least I had the confirmation that she was feeling better. Hell, that she was even alive.

Not seeing her wasn't going to be an option moving forward. Not unless we figured something else out with this bond. I had a feeling Dawsyn's solution to that would be to flat out reject me, but dragons didn't reject their mates. Even if they hated each other, the bond was sacred and I intended to treat it as such.

Even if finding her was poorly timed and I had the weight of saving an entire realm on my shoulders, I still wanted to keep Dawsyn just close enough.

The last couple of days had taught me that. How I could have thought I could leave her and go back to Drago alone was beyond me. Though, there wasn't a way I could bring her with me unless she accepted our bond with a blood exchange.

Something told me we were months, maybe even years, away from that happening. But I'd find a way to wait, because there was no walking away from her now. Dawsyn was going to be mine. There had to be a way to show her that having a mate wasn't the end of the world.

An hour later, I'd grown tired of sitting up in the tree I chose to hide in. Pitiful, I knew, but it was the only way to stay close to Dawsyn without her disappearing back to her room.

She'd stayed with River and a vampire I'd heard her call Justine, but I had never met or even paid attention to her before. As I watched River walk away to join some of the other guys who had come and gone from their group, I wondered if this was the time that I needed to make my appearance.

I wasn't normally one to stay quiet and put up with stupid shit, but Dawsyn was different, and I was trying to be different as well.

Even if that hadn't exactly been working out for me.

Justine grabbed her hand, and they joined a group of maybe ten others who were dancing about twenty feet from me.

Instead of going to her, I continued to wait like a fool. I

watched as her hands went up in the air and moved lightly over her caramel locks before trailing down over the hips that she shook. I wasn't the only one watching either.

Another shifter spotted her and moved in behind her. I expected Dawsyn to push him away, but she didn't immediately respond. Her eyes were closed, and she continued to dance, letting the shifter put his hands on her.

My nails turned to claws and dug into the branches I held on to. How could she do that? How could she let another touch her when she knew who I was?

Maybe I was more of a fool than I previously thought. Maybe I shouldn't have spent the last few days allowing my mind to believe that this could somehow work. Even if not now, but at some point in the future.

Dawsyn was eight years younger than me, but she wasn't a child. She was twenty-two, according to what I'd learned about her. She had no excuse for her behavior other than she truly didn't give a shit about finding her mate. About me.

Only those thoughts quickly evaporated when the shifter's hands moved more aggressively over Dawsyn's body, tugging at her shirt and forcing her to turn around.

When her eyes opened, they were wide and bright. She seemed confused and frozen in place as the guy moved his head closer to hers.

His hand wrapped around her neck, jerking her head closer. My eyes saw nothing else after that other than red.

Bloody, crimson red.

Whoever this shifter was, he was about to have my face burned into his memory.

That was only if he lived for much longer.

I jumped from the trees—still thinking rationally enough to keep the cloak around me up—and landed right beside them. A flash of flesh appeared in my peripherals, but I paid it no attention.

My fingers wrapped around the shifter's neck and easily lifted his six-foot-tall body from the ground. "Don't fucking touch her."

His voice was nothing more than a gargle. Still, my grip tightened. His legs kicked out, but even as he made contact with my shins, nothing was distracting me from wanting to murder the wolf shifter who thought he could put hands on my mate.

His green eyes blinked and widened. His cheeks reddened before they started going pale, and I gladly watched as he grew weaker by the second.

Until a force hit my spine and other sounds broke through my singular focus.

"Put him down, Cillian," Dawsyn demanded, striking me over and over again.

Without thinking twice, my fingers loosened and the piece of shit dropped unceremoniously to the ground in a tangled heap.

I turned to my mate, hands hovering over her shoulders. "Are you okay?"

She stepped closer, and I thought that meant she needed comfort, but instead, she looked up at me with pure hatred. "I was doing fucking fantastic until you stormed in. I never asked for you or...your help. I don't want it, so leave me the hell alone. Now and forever."

I'd thought the ache from not seeing her was an agony

unlike anything else, but the venom in her words and the sneer on her face was like a dagger to my heart.

Hope had made me tolerate her dislike of our situation, but seeing the hatred in her eyes? That changed everything.

Dawsyn wasn't ready for me, and there was a chance she might never be.

I knew I should walk away before doing so became so painful that I lost sight of why I was really here.

My realm needed me. If Dawsyn didn't, I needed to find a way to accept that.

Or I had to figure out how to fight for them both, but the mere thought of that seemed impossible.

A fissure shot through my chest, and fury scorched my veins.

Chapter Thirteen

DAWSYN

What in the shittery shit was that? My heart was racing, and my adrenaline felt like fire coursing through my body. One moment I'd been dancing by myself, and the next I'd been imagining that Cillian's hands were on me. I hadn't expected that to happen, but before I could dissect the information, I'd come face-to-face with a complete stranger.

Just as I'd been prepared to knock the handsy shifter on his ass, Cillian appeared out of nowhere and nearly killed the idiot.

I tried talking him down, but the dragon shifter had lost all sense of rationale, causing a scene and embarrassing me. It wasn't until I began punching his back that he finally paid attention to me.

He was going to get his ass found out and killed. As much as his existence annoyed me, I refused to carry that responsibility on my shoulders.

Yelling at him hadn't been my plan, but I was at my wits' end with the situation.

As soon as I'd told him that I didn't want him, something dark passed over his face. There was a swift change in his mood, as if he'd flipped a switch inside his head and all emotion fled from him.

When I expected him to argue with me, he simply pushed through the crowd we'd acquired and stormed away.

Rage filled my chest, and my hands clenched at my sides. Damn it. He had a way of pushing every single one of my buttons. Worse, I didn't even think he meant to.

A soft hand wrapped around my wrist. "We should go."

I looked up to find Justine's gaze moving between me and the people who were beginning to whisper a little too loudly about what had just transpired.

I let the vampire lead me from the party, taking the opposite route I assumed we would. With every step I took, the roar of my earlier headache became louder.

My fingers rubbed over my temples, and I swallowed thickly, hoping like hell I wasn't about to vomit in front of my new friend. "Where's River?"

"I think he went after Cillian," she said.

My head snapped up. "We have to find them."

River was strong, but I had no idea what the dragon shifter was capable of. Something told me it was a lot more than just being able to block his true identity. If River pushed him too far... I couldn't even think about something happening to my best friend without wanting to shift and disappear forever into the forest.

Justine didn't take my panic seriously. "They're big boys. Let them sort out whatever testosterone issues they're having."

Having this stupid dragon shifter secret was increasing my frustration daily.

My fingers rubbed against my temple as we went through the common area. I tried to scent out River or even the earthy scent I could usually associate with Cillian, but the further we walked, the worse I felt.

Not as bad as before, but still not great, which annoyed the shit out of me.

Only because you know why, my wolf finally chimed in. *Cillian being close was making you feel better.*

I chose not to respond to her. Instead, I tried to do small talk with Justine. "What classes are you enjoying most right now?"

She chuckled. "Seriously? That's what you want to talk about?"

I shrugged. "Got anything better?"

"Yeah. How about what you did to get Cillian's attention?" she asked. "Girls around here have been pining over him since he showed up almost a month ago. He's either ignored them or been an asshole."

"I never said he wasn't an asshole," I scoffed. "In fact, I'm pretty sure I said he *was*."

With my head all muddled, I wasn't actually sure about much, but I was positive I'd at least implied that little detail.

"Either way," I continued. "I don't want his attention, and I'm hoping he leaves me alone after this disaster."

As the words left my mouth, my chest twisted, aching like I was being stabbed.

This bond was definitely screwing with me.

Now that I was willing to admit that it was my connection with Cillian making me feel like shit, it was a little easier to ignore the ill feelings. At least until Justine continued to speak.

"I don't know why," she said. "He's like sex on a stick. You should at least sample the goods."

I practically choked on air. "I'm sorry. *What*?"

Her lips thinned in obvious disappointment. "Oh, come on. You're a wolf shifter. You have needs. I know you're not as innocent as you're trying to appear."

She wasn't wrong, but being the alpha's daughter also meant my selection of men was few and far between. I'd learned long ago to override my needs. At least until my heats started last year. That was unexpectedly brutal and a time in my life that my dad refused to acknowledge.

Before I had to talk about my sex life with the vampire, my phone buzzed in my back pocket. I was so nervous about who might be calling that I nearly dropped the damned thing on the sidewalk. When I finally got a look at the screen, it was Brixley calling and not River like I'd hoped.

"Hey, Brix," I said when I clicked answer. "How's it going?"

Brixley was a friend from Los Angeles. I'd known her since she was born, but we weren't as close as River and I were. Though, I wasn't sure if that was because of our age difference or because she preferred to keep to herself.

"Are you alone?" she asked instead of responding to my question.

"No, I'm walking back to the dorm with a friend. What's going on?"

"Call me when you're alone," she said, then hung up on me.

I glanced down at my screen, dumbfounded.

"Is everything okay?" Justine asked, even though I knew she'd heard every word that Brixley did and didn't really say.

"No clue." My speed increased, and any earlier pains I'd been feeling were replaced with the stress of wondering what the hell Brixley saw and what it had to do with me.

"Do you want me to come up with you?" Justine asked as we approached Baker House.

My head shook. "If you can go find River and Cillian, that would be better. Make sure they're not trying to kill each other, please."

She chuckled. "River is smarter than that. Cillian on the other hand... Nobody really knows there. Maybe I should find them."

With the mate bond and what I'd already learned about the dragon shifter, I didn't think Cillian would actually hurt River, who was practically my family, but I still needed to be sure after what I'd just said to him.

After saying goodbye to Justine, I raced up to my room and had the phone up to my ear before the door was unlocked.

"Are you alone now?" Brixley asked when she answered.

"Yep. What did you see?" The witch-wolf hybrid had acquired an extra sense of awareness when she was little that she has continued to hone. Nobody called her a seer since what she could "see" was sporadic and not exactly a vision, but she was never wrong when she felt something about the future.

"You're in danger," she said quietly. "I don't know why or who you need to be aware of, but someone isn't going to be happy about your existence."

"What the hell does that mean?" I asked. "I'm just a wolf shifter. Nothing special."

As the words tumbled out of my mouth, they felt like just another lie. Only I had no idea why.

Maybe I'd been on to something with wanting to research the Luna Marked on my own. It was what I'd been worried about before I'd become distracted with a dragon shifter mate.

"You might think that now, but I know what I felt, Dawsyn," she said with surety in her tense voice. "The bigger problem is you're not supposed to come home. I thought that might be the solution, but the more I dug into what I was sensing, the more I realized you're where you're supposed to be, but you're not safe, either."

Well, that wasn't helpful. Not one damned bit.

"So besides me being unsafe from unknown situations," I said, "is there anything else you can enlighten me with?"

Silence was my only response, and my stomach began to churn harder than it had over the last couple days.

"Brixley?" I said cautiously.

"It's too crazy," she whispered. "I want to help you, I'm just not sure I'm understanding everything correctly."

Shit. What other shitstorms was I about to find myself in the middle of?

"Nothing is too crazy for me," I assured her. "Maybe if you share with me, we can sort out the meaning together."

I could hear the wind blowing around her. She must have been hiding out in the forest of her pack where she still lived with her parents. Hopefully nobody had followed her, but she had a hard time telling since she didn't get a wolf, taking more after her mom than her dad.

Brixley let out a heavy sigh. "I'm seeing something...or someone...with fire and scales."

Son of a bitch. That was the last thing I expected her to say, but I could understand why she'd feel crazy if she was thinking about dragons. I wasn't going to lead her to that thought myself, though.

I shoved down my panic that someone else was close to learning Cillian's secret. Though, I didn't know why. I'd just told the dragon that I didn't want anything to do with him. I shouldn't care that his true identity was at risk.

I shouldn't, but I wasn't a fan of lying to myself, which meant I had to admit that I *did* care. More than I wanted to. And I wasn't sure if that was because of the bond or because deep down, I sensed that Cillian wasn't a bad person.

"After everything that's happened in our world, would you be surprised there was something scaley hiding out there?" I asked casually, hoping she had other ideas about this creature.

"I mean, a little? Maybe?" She paused. "Would you?"

My annoyance at the amount of lies stacking up around me was going to crush me at some point. I was certain of that. "Not really."

Her sigh was strangled. "But all I can think of are dragons. That's insane, right? How could *they* hide from us?"

And there was the D word I was hoping to avoid.

"What else did you see?" I asked, intent on changing the direction of the conversation.

"Dawsyn." Her tone was full of annoyance, telling me she saw more and my avoidance proved something I was hoping not to.

"What do you know about what I saw?" she demanded. "If you know something, then it could help me make sense of the rest of this."

Damn it. She was right, but I'd promised Cillian I wouldn't tell. Though technically, I wasn't breaking the news of dragon shifters if she'd already come to that conclusion.

Yeah, I liked that, and my chest didn't tighten with guilt when I put it that way. Hell, maybe this would only help Cillian, having Brixley's knowledge.

"Dragon shifters are real," I said quietly. "At least one of them is."

I could hear her sharp intake of breath. "I knew it. I just didn't want to admit it. People already think I'm crazy enough."

My brows pinched together. "What does that mean?" Sure, I wasn't close with her, but that didn't mean I cared about her any less. If people were screwing with her, I was going to do something about it.

"Nothing," she insisted. "We need to figure this out. So, we know they're real now, and I know you need to stay where you are, but why?"

I was torn between forcing her to tell me what was going on and admitting that I knew why I was supposed to be here, which annoyed me immensely. I no longer felt as if coming to Mystics Academy was my idea.

Fate had intervened. I was here just mere weeks after Cillian showed up. That couldn't be a coincidence.

"First, I'll let go of the subject of your troubles as long as you promise to come to me if things get out of hand. Also promise me that you'll remember what a badass you are. Whatever people are saying, they're just doing so because they're jealous of how amazing you are as not only a witch hybrid, but as a person."

She chuckled and sniffled at the same time. "I promise. To both things."

"Good," I said with a grin. "Now, what I'm about to tell you cannot be shared with anyone. Actually, none of this conversation can be. Not with your parents or even the squirrels in the trees. Do you understand?"

"I do," she replied quickly.

"Alright, then." I paused, listening for signs of anyone that might be too close to my room, but found none. "Dragons are real, one is here at the academy with me, and he's my fated mate."

Brixley began to laugh, the sound turning almost manic. "Of *course* he is, because crazy shit like this only happens to our families."

She wasn't wrong.

"There's more," I said. "Something is wrong with his realm—that's where the dragons live like the fae do in theirs—and he's here to find a solution."

A somberness settled over her quickly. "What happens when he goes back?"

I knew what she was asking: Would I disappear with him?

"I don't know," I admitted. "I told him I didn't want a mate."

"You rejected him?" she gaped. "I don't understand. What I'm sensing with all this… It doesn't add up."

"What do you mean?" I asked. "Did you know I'd found my mate?"

She was silent for what felt like hours instead of seconds. "Not until now, but as soon as you said that, something else started to form with the other images."

"What?" I demanded, my back tense and eyes squeezed closed.

If Brixley saw me with Cillian, I couldn't deny that would change things.

"I see you taking a mate," she said reverently, "but he's a chosen mate. Not a fated one."

Anguish threatened to swallow me. Yes, I'd wanted to reject Cillian, but knowing this and wishing for it were two different things.

A chosen mate over a fated one that my wolf had been connected to in a past life? Was I that stubborn and awful to hurt both of them like that? Gods, I hoped fucking not. Regardless of what I'd just said to him at the party.

I'd expected Brix to give me clarity, but by the way my heart burned with grief for a bond we'd never even accepted, I was worse off than I'd been five minutes ago.

Even worse, I had no idea what I was supposed to do next.

Chapter Fourteen

CILLIAN

The further I walked away from Dawsyn, the more furious I became. I thought I could find a way to accept her rejection, but she'd dismissed me so easily. I'd only been trying to help, and she'd insulted me. In front of everyone.

I wasn't okay with that, and neither was my dragon.

He was hurt more than angry, but at least he was understanding now that this just might not be our mate, regardless of what fate thought.

I was headed in the direction of the south forest, wanting to get far enough away from the party so that I could shift, but I only made it as far as Rainier Hall before River caught up with me.

Part of me expected him to punch first and ask questions later, especially after our talk in front of their room. Hell, I even hoped for him to hit me so that I could feel something other than the loss of Dawsyn, but he surprisingly remained mostly calm.

"What the hell was that?" he demanded, stance wide and eyes bright under the star-filled sky.

"It was what needed to be done," I answered. "Why weren't you watching her to make sure nothing like that happened?"

He laughed right in my face. "You've met Dawsyn, right? She doesn't need me to watch her. She could have put Jude right on his ass for touching her if she wanted. It didn't seem like that was the case before you felt the need to step in."

My chest rumbled, and I had to curl my fingers in before my nails turned to sharp claws. "She doesn't want him."

"Maybe so, but more importantly, she doesn't want *you*," he taunted. "Why don't you accept that and just leave her alone?"

My blood pressure rose, and my vision flickered. Hearing another person say my mate didn't want me flipped a switch inside me that I'd yet to touch.

The previous rumble turned into a menacing growl and I stepped forward until I was right in River's face. "She's *my* mate."

I didn't mean for the words to come out. I meant to tell him that she'd change her mind eventually, even though I'd just told myself that it didn't matter if she did. Clearly, I'd been wrong.

River's face paled. "She's your what?"

"Nothing," I said, backing up. "I'll leave Dawsyn alone. Message received."

He reached for my arm when I turned away, stopping

my movements. "No, I heard you loud and clear. You're Dawsyn's *fated* mate?"

"I didn't say that," I grumbled.

"You pretty much did," he said. "Holy shit. That's why she was so sick. She's rejecting you."

Fuck. Hearing him point that out so candidly wasn't helping my mood. I jerked my arm out of his grip and took a few more steps back, but still faced him. For his safety, there needed to be more space between us.

"What was wrong with her?" I asked after taking a few deep breaths.

He shook his head. "Yeah, I'm not going there with you. You need to back up a minute. When did you find out that you were mates?"

I wasn't comfortable with this conversation. From my understanding, River was Dawsyn's best friend—like a brother to her—which was why I hadn't lost my shit about her living with him to begin with.

If she hadn't told him yet, I didn't think it was my place to. Though I'd already spilled one of the more important parts, maybe she wouldn't be as pissed off if I kept the rest to myself.

"You're going to need to talk to Dawsyn about that," I said. "I'm trying to leave her alone. I kept away while she holed up in the dorm, and I only meant to watch from a distance tonight. I didn't expect to have to intervene."

"You didn't 'have to' do anything," River countered. "You chose to make a fool of yourself in front of everyone and embarrassed Dawsyn, but I guess I can understand why. Or at least attempt to." He paused and then seemed to talk more to himself than me. "A mate. I never would have guessed."

When he'd said, "embarrass Dawsyn," her ire toward me started to make more sense. I'd brought attention to her and, from what I'd seen, she preferred to stay out of the spotlight. Though, the hope I had been feeling that maybe she didn't mean what she'd said about me leaving her alone—that she'd only lost her temper—felt fleeting now that I was seeing things differently.

"Listen, I appreciate that you're so protective of Dawsyn," I said. "Just know, I'm not going to hurt her. I'll leave her alone as best I can while I finish doing what I came here for, but that's not always going to be possible until we figure out the rest."

The more time that passed, the more I was able to think without being so inundated with rage, and the more I was set on fighting for my mate. If she wanted to break our connection, she was going to have to figure that out on her own. I wouldn't help make any part of that easy on her, no matter how much she tried to hurt me.

That might make me even more of an asshole in her eyes, but I wasn't a quitter. There was no more debating between choosing Dawsyn or my realm. I'd find a way to have them both. I refused to let Dawsyn go easily, even if I had no idea how we could make it work.

I wouldn't leave my realm to die and she didn't seem like the type to walk away from her family here, but that didn't mean the situation was impossible. The odds just weren't great.

River shoved his hands in his front pockets and looked me right in the eyes. "I need to go. I won't stop you from seeing Dawsyn like before, but if she refuses, then I'll protect her until my dying breath. I'm not afraid of you, Cillian."

And I knew he wasn't, but not because he was stronger than me. He just cared so much for Dawsyn that he didn't give a shit if he got his ass beat. He would still try to keep her safe.

"Are you going to tell her I told you about the mate bond?" I asked him.

I wanted to be prepared if she was going to be even angrier with me.

"I haven't decided yet," he replied. "I'm sure you'll know if I do."

The smirk on his face told me he was looking forward to that little show.

"See you later, Cillian," River said, strutting past me, acting as if he didn't have a care in the world.

I DIDN'T HEAR ANYTHING FROM DAWSYN THE REST of the night, and I slept like shit, which meant I was up early and searching for any information that might help Drago survive whatever was attacking it.

Nannio had told me I needed a spell to locate the energy, but so far, the only "locating" spells I had stumbled upon were for people and things, not magic, which was what we assumed we were dealing with.

I tried mind-linking with my grandmother again to ask her some follow-up questions, but of course, she didn't respond.

The fact that she'd sent me away and had been dodging most of my attempts at contact made me believe she'd sent me here without telling me everything I'd needed to know. It made me want to go home even more, but instead, I found myself heading toward Professor Hayes' office. He was the one teacher who previously dismissed me when I tried to speak with him, but I wasn't going to relent this time.

My knuckles knocked on the wooden door, and I could hear papers rustling around inside, along with even breathing.

He was probably grading tests and didn't want to be disturbed, but I didn't really care. He was the only professor with a history in origin magic. I'd tried to talk to him twice before, but the first time we'd been interrupted and the second, he barely even looked me in the eyes, thanks to stacks of papers on his desk, and yelled to be left alone.

"Come in," a grumbly voice called out. One that was hopefully only *grumbly* from lack of use and not because he was already in a mood.

I opened and closed the door behind me, then took a seat in the only chair in front of his desk, which was made of cold metal and not at all welcoming for his students.

The rest of the room was chaos. Pictures hung off-center, unlabeled boxes stacked on top of each other and several more opened, but filled with papers that didn't seem to be in any sort of order.

"I've seen you before, but you're not one of my students," he said pointedly.

I smirked at him. "No, you declined my entry to your class."

"If you're here to plead for another decision, you're wasting both of our time." He picked his pen back up and gave his attention to the paper he was likely grading based on the red marks all over it.

"I just have a few questions. If you'll take five minutes to answer them, I won't have another reason to bother you," I said, staring at the top of his receding hairline.

He made a gurgling sound, but still didn't look back up at me.

"I'm a hybrid, and I don't know my father," I said, deciding to just speak since he hadn't banished me from his office yet. "He was a warlock, and his last name was Bishop. I was hoping you could tell me about the founding witch families and books left behind from them."

His eyes still didn't meet mine, but he did pause the movement of his pen. "And you assume that since he claimed the name Bishop that he was linked to the original family?"

"According to my mother before she died, he was," I said with an air of confidence I shouldn't have since every word was a lie.

The professor still didn't look up at me. "I can't help you."

"Yet you claim to have the most knowledge on our founding families."

He flicked his gaze up to me. "Let me rephrase: I won't help you."

"Why not?" I asked, remaining calm, regardless of how much I wanted to let my dragon tear his head off.

An annoyed sigh escaped him, and he dropped his pen onto the desk. "Because I don't want to. But if you're insistent about finding answers, then I suggest you go to the fourth floor of the library and find the section on original vampires."

Confusion hit me at the center of my chest. "I don't understand."

"Because you're not who you say, or think, you are," he countered. "If you know what you're looking for, then it will make sense. Otherwise, you don't really need to know the information you seek. Now get out of my office."

I stood and gave him my back, not seeing the point in thanking him for his time when he didn't really want to give it to me.

I was tempted to ask what he meant by "you're not who you say, or think, you are," but I withheld. I knew who I was, and I wasn't going to push him into wanting to dig further into my background. One that didn't exist in this place.

Though, I was curious enough about his recommendation to go back to the library. I'd been on the fourth floor when Dawsyn had found me before and never had the chance to go through the rest of the shelves. Even if I had, I probably would have skipped over the vampires.

Now, I had a reason not to.

Leaving the admin building, I used the back exit that kicked me out into the common area. I took two steps toward the library that was to the right of the park-like setting, then stopped abruptly.

Dawsyn.

She was here somewhere. I could smell her sweet scent, and there was no chance of me walking any further without getting eyes on her.

I glanced casually to my left. The longer it took me to find her in the morning crowds, the tenser my shoulders became.

Finally, my eyes landed on her back. She was bundled up, and her body was curved in on itself, but suddenly, she stiffened and her head snapped up.

Bruno handed her the drink she seemed to be waiting for, then she slowly turned around.

I held my breath for those few seconds it took for her eyes to land on me. She'd known I was behind her and hadn't walked in the opposite direction.

Instead, she blinked and took a step toward me. The action should have made me feel better, but something told me that Dawsyn and I were a long way from having any *good* conversations.

Chapter Fifteen

DAWSYN

Just my luck. Cillian was in the common area. I considered ignoring him and taking the long way home, but after talking with Brixley, I spent the rest of the night thinking about what I wanted.

Was my newfound freedom more important than my long-term happiness? Did it have to be? Could I have both? There was a chance that I didn't need to choose between the life I was searching for and the one that had found me. Realizing that, I thought maybe Cillian wasn't just the fated mate I knew him to be, but that he could possibly be the one I chose one day.

Though, a shit-ton of fear was preventing me from settling on any one answer. I thought about all the what-ifs and wondered if Brixley was wrong, even though her visions had never been before. When she was three, she had predicted her mom was going to have another child before he was even conceived.

Whatever the answer was, the one thing I was certain of

was that I was where I was supposed to be, and that Cillian wasn't going anywhere until he figured out his mess.

Maybe what I was supposed to do was help him. He could go back to his realm, our bond would fizzle out, dragons could stay hidden if they decided, and I would then later—hopefully not until I was ready—find my chosen mate as Brixley said.

That was the scenario that made me the least crazy inside, so I was going with it for now. At least trying to. Any time I thought too hard about it, my wolf snarled, disagreeing with me. Though, she'd since stopped talking to me, so her opinions were quickly becoming invalid.

The only time I didn't sense disapproval from her was when I considered Brixley was right and wrong. That the danger I was in was because I was trying to reject Cillian, and this chosen mate...the idea of who he could be wasn't helping.

Because that option was much too complicated for me to consider at the moment, I'd ignored it as best I could and kept my mind on the former option, the one that had me doing whatever I could to help Cillian save his realm and get him back home. That was why I was making my way toward him after getting my coffee.

If he was out here, then I assumed he was looking for me or answers. I was going to try to at least give him one of those things.

Damn him, though. The closer I got to him, the more I inhaled his earthy scent. It had gooseflesh appearing on my skin and my stomach tightening with need. His dark hair was a mess, but a sexy one, and his mouth... I didn't even want to think about what I'd allowed myself to imagine those lips doing to me the night before.

Even while I was furious with him for being an alpha male, I still thought he was "sex on a stick," as Justine had called him.

My wolf perked up briefly, but she still didn't seem to be talking to me. I could only sense her excitement at being near our mate.

I really did feel bad for hurting her. She'd been my other half since I was born. Not agreeing on something so significant wasn't common, but I had to be true to myself. If I wasn't ready for a mate and Cillian needed to save his realm, we weren't right for each other. It was as simple as that.

At least, that was what I was going to keep telling myself.

"Good morning," his deep voice practically purred when I was within a few feet of him.

"Morning," I replied, sipping my coffee. I was tempted to bring up the night before right away, but a part of me hoped he understood that he'd crossed a line and was willing to admit that.

"About last night..."

I fought a smirk. At least the man was smart.

"I can't leave you alone."

I blinked several times. No apology? No "I shouldn't have...insert all the stupid things he did."

"Excuse me?" I lightly stuttered, gripping the cup in my hand harder.

He stepped closer, breathing me in, and tilting his face closer to mine. "You might not be ready for a mate, but you're still *my* mate. I was going to walk away and give you what you want, but I can't do that. I won't lie to myself. I want you, Dawsyn."

Mother fucking shit.

I should have just taken the long way back to my dorm.

"No." That was all I could think to say. I didn't know how to tell him that this just wasn't going to happen. I wasn't going to be his mate. Well, at least not officially. There wouldn't be a special bond between us. Not now. Not ever.

He chuckled and grinned at me. "I thought you'd still feel that way. Don't worry, I've been learning how to be a patient man, Dawsyn. I also have my realm to consider. I can focus on that while you take your time doing whatever it is that you need to do, but I don't accept your rejection."

This stupid, stupid dragon. I wanted to...

My eyes briefly closed, and the images were nowhere near as aggressive as I wanted them to be, which only served to increase my frustration.

When I looked back up at him, he was still smiling. "Your cheeks are flushed."

Thanks, Captain Obvious.

I let out a sharp huff of annoyance. "Yeah, because you're pissing me off and I don't want to make a scene."

His responding chuckle sent shivers down my spine. "Right. Well, I got a lead this morning to check out the vampire history books. Do you want to join me in the library again?"

That reminded me of how Bruno had already known I was there with Cillian before, mere minutes after I'd left. Given how last night went, I didn't need more people talking about me with Cillian, but I also really wanted the dragon shifter to be gone.

I was tempted to stomp my feet like a child, but I refrained and begrudgingly agreed to go with him. "Sure. I don't have anything better to do this morning."

His hand gripped his chest dramatically. "Oh, how you wound me."

Who was this man, and where did the grumpy one go? I'd take *grumpy* over *persistent* any day of the week.

"Do you actually want my help?" I asked instead of playing into his...whatever this was.

"I do."

I pointed a finger at him and made a figure-eight over his chest. "Then, don't be whatever this is. I've already told you what I want. I get that you don't agree and there's not much I can do about that, but there has to be a middle ground. Once you find what you need, were you really expecting me to go back to Drago with you? Or are the... Or is your family planning on moving here?"

I realized a few seconds too late that I should probably be more careful with what I say and where. It seemed people around here were always being watched.

"I don't know what the plan is, and I don't have any expectations, Dawsyn." I was pretty sure he had more to say, but I had to interrupt him.

"Quit saying my name like that." He'd repeated it several times this morning. More than he had in any previous interaction. The way the syllables rolled off his tongue... It wasn't like he had a heavy accent or anything, but damn it. I didn't like the way my body responded to it, begging to be pressed against his as he whispered my name over and over into my ear.

"Am I getting under your skin, Dawsyn?" he asked with the evilest of smirks.

Because I wasn't thinking right, I took his bait and shoved him hard. The same spark appeared, and then my hands covered my mouth. I was going to get him found out.

His shield seemed to only fall for a second before he had it back up. I could feel the mate bond wrap around me in that brief moment, warming my insides and making me want to put my hands on him. To taste every inch of him and...

Nope. I wasn't going there.

I had a plan, and I was going to stick to that, damn it.

"Library. Now," I demanded. My hand nearly grabbed his to drag him along, but I caught myself at the last second, then stormed past him.

Maybe helping Cillian wasn't the best idea I could have come up with, but whatever. I'd just have to figure out how to stop myself from feeling the full force of our bond and how to keep my mind from conjuring inappropriate images of him kneeling before me, using his tongue for all kinds of wicked things.

Yeah. That was going to be super easy to do.

We arrived at the library, and I started heading up the stairs, assuming we were headed to where I'd found him before.

He reached for me when we were on the second floor, placing his palm at the base of my back. Tension shot through me, and I sucked in a sharp breath, pausing all my movements. "What are you doing?" I hissed.

"Slowing you down," he said. "You're drawing attention, and that's the last thing we need right now."

Ha! He drew attention simply by existing, but I didn't need to stroke his ego by telling him that.

"Right," I relented. "You lead the way then."

If he was in front of me, then I would be forced to slow down and—

"If you wanted a better view, all you had to do was ask," he whispered teasingly.

Oh, I was going to kill him.

Before I could retort, he was four steps ahead of me. I calmly followed him to the fourth floor—keeping my eyes averted from his firm ass as much as possible—and we went right instead of left toward where he was before.

"You mentioned vampires, right?" Maybe we could split up and get twice the work done in half the time. Getting back to my dorm sooner rather than later seemed like the safest thing.

He glanced around and nodded. "Professor Hayes told me to look there."

"Does he know about..."

"I don't think so," he answered, but didn't sound very confident. "I was asking about original families."

I was supposed to be helpful in order to get Cillian back to his realm and my life back to normal, but I wasn't sure how *helpful* I wanted to be. Bringing people into this situation who were like family to me didn't seem like the brightest idea, especially when I wanted this whole mate thing to stay between Cillian and me as much as possible. Yet...

"I know an original line vampire," tumbled out of my mouth.

He raised a brow. "How?"

"Well, I call her Aunt Amersyn, but I've known her since I was born. She and her mate are the leaders of the guards around the communities."

"How is your aunt a vampire?" His voice was full of confusion, and I almost considered screwing with him, but decided better of it.

"She's not my blood aunt," I answered. "She's been part of my family for years. My parents and her, along with a few others, are the reason the communities started to form and hybrids became a thing."

"Is that why you can stay with River?" he asked. "Because your parents are famous?"

I shrugged. "Are we here to talk about me? I only mentioned Amersyn in case you need more help than what we're able to find. If you don't, then forget I said anything." I pointed to the back shelf. "I'll start over here."

Before he could respond or even object, I walked away. Space was needed immediately.

My feelings toward the dragon shifter were already softening again, and that was the last thing I needed. Once he was gone, I'd feel normal again and my wolf would understand this was the best choice.

Until then, I needed to make physical distance a top priority with Cillian.

Chapter Sixteen

CILLIAN

Changing my attitude toward Dawsyn had been more insightful than I realized it would be. My forwardness showed me exactly what I wanted to know.

I affected Dawsyn. A lot more than she wanted to admit, but also couldn't deny.

I wouldn't take advantage of the pull from the bond. Forcing her to accept me was the last thing I wanted, even if the fates thought we were meant for each other. But that didn't mean I was walking away like I'd considered before.

For the time being, I would keep her as close as she'd allow and show her that her life didn't have to end just because we were mates.

Of course, I didn't know how that was going to work when the world didn't know I existed in my true form. I couldn't remain hidden forever if I stayed here, but that was a problem to sort out later.

For now, having Dawsyn close in any capacity was good enough.

I also needed to chat with River. It didn't seem as if he'd

told her he knew about the bond. I assumed if he had said something to her that she would have yelled at me. I'd been prepared for that, but when she'd offered to help me, I wasn't going to ruin the opportunity to spend more time with her.

Well, at least to be in the same room with her.

After our little conversation, she'd stayed as far from me as possible, only coming to me when she found something that might interest me. Even then, she'd drop the book on the nearest table and go back to her corner.

Three hours later, she came back to me empty handed. "I can't focus on the words when I'm this hungry. I'll be back later."

I raised a brow. "You're not going to invite me to lunch?"

"You're a big boy," she quipped. "If you're hungry, I assume you know where the dining hall is."

She whirled around on one foot and headed toward the stairs. I watched the sway of her hips, the swish of her caramel hair, and even the length of her stride as she increased the distance between us.

I gave her a head start, letting her think that I wasn't going to follow. While I waited to leave, I gathered the books we'd found and set them on a shelf so that they hopefully wouldn't be messed with while we were gone.

Once that was done, I headed out and toward the common area, assuming that she was going to eat at the dining hall since she'd mentioned it. *Shit*. She could have gone back to her dorm. People kept food in their small fridges all the time.

Deciding not to waste time worrying, I kept in the

direction I was already headed. With quick steps, I passed by other students, not looking at more than the ground as I went. I didn't have time for potential conversations.

When I got to the doors of the dining hall, I shoved the left one open and my gaze raised, scanning the food line. She wasn't there and I almost turned right around, but her scent caught my attention above all the others mixed inside the building.

There she was, at the drink station.

Instead of going right to her, I moved to the line and got my own food. A steak sandwich, side of beans, and chips. The academy at least fed us well. Hell, it was better than I'd eaten most days back in Drago.

Grabbing a bottle of water last, I scanned the tables and found Dawsyn's eyes on me. She was seated in the far corner. Alone. Like she knew I'd join her and she was okay with that.

I took the unspoken invitation and headed toward her. Eyes followed me as I went, and I realized then that I maybe should have rethought my goal of pushing people away by being an asshole. I'd only attracted more attention, which was the last thing I needed when time was running out for Drago and I needed to convince Dawsyn that being my mate wasn't the end of the world.

When I approached her table, I set the tray down and took my seat. Without looking at her or saying a word, I lifted my sandwich and took a massive bite, moaning around the meat and bread. "Hmmm."

"You know you're not the only one sitting here, right?" she chastised.

I finally glanced up at her, a half grin on my face since

my mouth was still full of food. "Oops." I gargled, then finished chewing.

She rolled her eyes and stabbed her tater tots with a fork, but didn't eat one. Instead, she abandoned the fork and picked up the burrito on her plate, shoving half of it in her mouth.

Her cheeks filled as the food was forced into her mouth, then she chewed silently, keeping my stare the whole time with one brow cocked up.

"Classy," I deadpanned.

She wiped the edges of her mouth with her middle finger, then spoke. "I'm not out to impress anyone here, Cillian. Least of all you. This is how I prefer to eat. If you don't like it, go sit somewhere else."

"Why did you choose this table?" I asked her.

She took another big bite, making me wait for her answer. Though, I wasn't sure if that was to annoy me or to come up with a lie.

"Because I'm not actually a student here," she said, a bit of sauce on her chin from that last bite. "I don't want to take someone's normal spot and have them bitch about it. I don't have time for petty drama."

"But you have time to help me save my realm," I countered.

The smirk on her face didn't bode well for me. "That is more helping myself, I assure you."

She could spout that bullshit all she wanted. Even though our bond was far from solidified, I could still sense how I made her feel. Even if she didn't like it, I affected her, and it wasn't just because I pissed her off.

She wanted *me*.

Not enough to give in to her desires, but like I'd told her before, I was learning to be a patient man. I would wait her out.

"What are you going to do if you can't find what you're looking for soon?" she asked me, her voice filled with more curiosity than snark.

"I don't know," I answered honestly. "Things are getting worse...back home. My grandmother doesn't want me to return until I have what I need, but I don't think I can wait much longer after hearing the last update from her."

She set her burrito down, wiped her face with a napkin, then folded her hands beneath her chin, golden-streaked hair falling in her face. "Is she your only family?"

My head shook. "I have an uncle, too. My mom died and my father disappeared into the dark forest when that happened."

She raised both brows. "What is the dark forest? I mean, I get the gist of it by the name, but how can someone disappear there?"

I chuckled lightly, not because of my father's disappearance, but because I was suddenly remembering what we were told as kids to prevent us from venturing too far north.

"As children, they told us there were shadows in the dark forest that would swoop us up and carry us off to another world," I said. "When I was old enough to know better, I learned that there was a different kind of weather system out there. Storms could rage in the dark forest, but everywhere else, it would be bright blue skies."

She smirked. "You went out there anyway, didn't you?"

I had, but not for the reasons she was going to expect. "Not often, but I had to as I was growing up or I could have hurt a lot of people."

Her face sobered, and she looked around us. "I want to ask more questions, but this probably isn't the right place."

No, it wasn't, and I needed to be more careful with what I said in public. I'd almost just told her about my lightning abilities, and anyone could have heard. It was uncomfortably easy to talk to her, which was something I had to be cautious with.

"Are you going to come back to the library with me after lunch?" I asked. We were a long way from being done in there, and I still hadn't found what Professor Hayes suggested I might.

She shrugged. "I need to talk to River. He went straight to his room last night after the party."

This was my opportunity to come clean. I should tell her that he already knows about us being mates, but I really didn't want to deal with a pissed-off Dawsyn right now. Not when we'd just had a civil, albeit short, conversation.

She could yell at me later.

I took the last bite of my sandwich. "I guess I'll see you around, then?"

Her shoulders deflated, and she rubbed her hands over her face. "Listen, I know I'm making this complicated, but no matter what I say or do, I really do want to help you. Do I like that I have to lie to those around me? No, but I have a pack. I know how important an entire community is."

Her words were said to likely make me feel better, but they didn't. Sure, I appreciated her empathy, but I'd rather have her help me because she felt a connection between us.

Not because the sooner I had my answers, the sooner I was going to be out of her life and gone saving my realm.

"Thanks for understanding," I said.

I'd done enough poking at her for the day. I could resume later, whenever she returned to punish me for telling River about our bond.

That was probably the only thing I was sure about when it came to my mate.

She hadn't finished her food, but she stood and walked away without saying another word or offering a smile.

Fighting for her wasn't going to be easy. I had a feeling I was going to be tortured every step of the way, but I also knew that if I got my way, my efforts would be more than worth any annoyance or pain I'd feel in the interim.

Dawsyn Chase was stubborn and outspoken and difficult, but she was my mate. I would get under that thick skin of hers if it was the last thing I did.

Chapter Seventeen

DAWSYN

Walking away from Cillian only continued to get more uncomfortable. Not in the way I was before when I'd been sick, but more so that I was becoming more and more confused. My only saving grace was that he was forced to have a shield up.

That shield muddled the bond between us.

Now that I knew there was a connection between us, I could sense the thrum of the tether when I was close to him, but it was more like a gentle whisper compared to the a loud, obnoxious roar I'd experienced when I'd shoved him and he'd accidentally dropped the cloak he'd created.

I meant what I'd said to him about helping with his problem, but I was beginning to second-guess everything. Again. It annoyed the fuck out of me.

I knew that if I continued to be around him, there was no way to avoid getting to know him. That was a huge risk. It seemed dumb as shit to think of falling for my fated mate as a risk, but damn it, I'd felt so certain I knew the direction I wanted to take my life before meeting him.

Now I was second-guessing every possibility and wondering if one of the other options I'd considered before might be better. Why not play sides and be mature about things? I wasn't stubborn enough to deny that I hadn't been feeling much joy since leaving my pack. There had been a lot of frustration and sickness and annoyance, but not so much of the excitement I'd been expecting.

Though, there might have been if I hadn't met Cillian.

Mother fucking shit. I didn't normally have to figure these things out on my own. I'd always had my wolf or River or even my mom and aunts to talk things through with.

Worse, this was so much bigger than me, but it seemed all I had was myself.

Just what I'd been saying I wanted. Yet, this felt pretty fucking terrible.

That should have been answer enough for me, and maybe it was, but as I approached Baker House, I did my best to shove the conflicted emotions down. I didn't want to bring them home with me when I couldn't talk to River about them.

When I made it inside the dorm, he was sitting at the small table with two books opened in front of him and a notebook with his pen in hand. He glanced up at me and smiled, but it didn't quite reach his eyes. "Hey."

"Hey, yourself," I said, grabbing the second chair and taking a seat across from him. "What are you studying?"

"Shadow vampires," he replied, but didn't look up from his book.

I peeked over at the pages. "I thought those didn't actually exist."

"Just because we don't see them doesn't mean they don't exist," he said. "They were here once, and they could come back at any time. Guards need to know how to be ready for them."

His tone was filled with irritation, and he still wasn't really looking up at me. My hand waved over the book closest to him. "What's up with you, Beastie? I didn't get to talk to you after the party or see you before class. Did something happen between the thing with Cillian and when you got home?"

"Nope."

Yeah, that wasn't going to work for me.

I got up and rudely sat on his books. "Talk to me, River."

"Why?" he snapped, finally staring at my face. "You haven't been talking to me."

I jerked back, not expecting that kind of...accusatory tone to lace his sharp words.

"What does that mean?" I asked hesitantly.

The only secret I'd kept from him was about Cillian and there was no way he could have known about that unless... Brixley.

"Did you talk to Brixley?" I demanded.

He shoved out of his seat. "*Brixley* knows? That's just wonderful. I didn't realize the two of you had grown so close while I'd been at school."

Hell, what did River know if not about Cillian? Or think he knew...

He shoved out of his chair and brushed past me toward his room, but I wasn't letting him get away that easily.

I ran in front of him, blocking his path. "Tell me what

you're talking about."

He laughed, but there was no smile on his face. "Do you have more than one secret right now, D? If not, then you should know. Otherwise, I'm not going to make this easy on you."

Technically, I had two. I knew dragons existed and that Cillian was my mate. Would he really be pissed at me for not telling him about dragons? Annoyed, sure. This though... Whatever he knew was personal, which meant he knew Cillian was my mate.

He must have figured it out last night during the public argument I had with Cillian or afterward.

Oh, that bastard dragon shifter. He wouldn't have. Would he?

"Did Cillian tell you that we're mates?" I asked pointedly, crossing my arms.

"Did Cillian tell..." he mocked, then sneered. "What do you think?"

I was going to kill that not-mate of mine. *Damn him!* And after I'd promised and kept his secret. Well, mostly. It wasn't my fault Brixley found out and he didn't even know about that, so this couldn't be some sort of sick payback.

"It's not that I didn't want to tell you, Riv," I pleaded. "It's just complicated."

"And you didn't think I could help," he said, this time with betrayal in his voice, which gutted me.

It was never my intention to upset River. Seeing the slump in his shoulders, pain in his eyes, and flattening of his lips, I knew I'd done just that.

"This isn't something anyone can help me with," I said, grabbing his hand and pulling him to the couch. "I don't want a mate. Most of all Cillian. I thought if I told people, that would only complicate things. He's only here for a short time. My hope was that he'd accept my rejection, leave, and the bond would just go away."

I also suspected that I'd have to do some work to make that bond bit happen, but that wasn't something I had stressed myself out with just yet.

We sat down on the couch, but River kept at least a foot of space between us. "So he'd leave and you'd never have to tell anyone, not even your best friend, that you'd met your fated mate?"

Well, when he put it that way, I sounded like the worst best friend ever.

"I'm not going to apologize for doing what I thought was best for me," I replied. "I'm sorry you're hurt because of it, but that wasn't my intention. If the situation had gotten out of control, then I'm sure I would have told you."

His chest rumbled. "You think Cillian nearly killing Jude last night wasn't 'the situation' getting out of control? Honestly, D. I expected better from you."

Well, that fucking burned.

"And I expected better of you," I snapped. "This is my problem, and while I appreciate that you would have preferred to be in the loop from the start and help me, I also hoped that you'd have respected my choice to handle this on my own."

He snorted and looked away from me. "Just like you do everything else."

"What the hell does that mean?" I was trying to be nice because I had hurt him, but fuck that nonsense. "You know what? I don't need to know. I don't deserve this."

I moved to get up, and he swirled around, freezing me in place with the glare he was casting my way. "*You* don't deserve this? How about *I* don't deserve to have the best friend I invited to come stay with me when she had nowhere else to go when she wanted out of her pack to show up here and act as if she can do whatever she wants now that she's left the watchful eyes of Mommy and Daddy?"

My chest hollowed as if he'd punched me. River and I had been in a lot of fights over the years, but this was... This was taking things too far.

I stood up the rest of the way, looking right at him even though he refused to meet my gaze. "I'm going to go before we say more things that we can't take back. Maybe we can sort this out later in a more adult way."

"Because keeping secrets is the adult way," he muttered.

I ignored him and headed out the door. We were both pissed. I would do my damnedest not to hold his previous words against him, but damn him. He'd cut deep, not even trying to understand the position I was in or how I was feeling.

Frustration began to fill me. Even though I refused to take my aggressions out on River, there was one shifter I had no problem showing my irritations to.

Cillian was going to know how much he fucked up. Really freaking soon.

I went straight to his room and tapped calmly on the door. With my foot tapping, I stood there and knocked several more times, but there were no noises from the other side and no answer.

Deciding to try option two, I made my way to the

library. He was hopefully there. Otherwise, he was going to be in class somewhere, but something told me he didn't attend class as often as he was supposed to.

I kept my head down and my hands shoved in the pockets of my jeans as I stormed across the school. Of course, the library had to be the furthest student building from our dorm.

Thankfully, I didn't see anyone I knew and made it there in record time. Only I hadn't entered quietly, letting the door slam shut behind me.

Several eyes glared up at me from studying students. I merely shrugged and headed toward the stairs.

One heavy inhale told me he was upstairs. I might not have been able to sense our mate bond from this distance, but his masked scent was—unfortunately—getting easier to pick out of a crowd.

What are you going to do? my wolf asked nervously.

Now *you want to talk to me?*

Yeah, I wasn't going to answer her. She could just figure it out like Cillian was about to.

I stormed onto the fourth floor, hair blowing behind me, fists clenched, and jaw tight. My eyes searched in the direction we'd been earlier, and there he was, sitting at the table with a stack of books around him. Calm as a cucumber who didn't know he was about to become smashed pickles.

He briefly glanced up and then did a double take, closing the book he was reading and standing up with his palms out. "I can explain."

My finger shook at him. "No talking. Get your ass outside."

"Why?" he asked, remaining where he was.

I leaned over the table and grabbed a handful of his black t-shirt between my fingers. "Because I'm going to kick your ass and don't want to damage any of the books in the process."

He looked down, brow raised and head cocked. "Are you challenging me?"

"Yep." I let the 'p' pop loudly. "Do you accept?"

He chuckled. "Do I have a choice?"

I didn't bother to answer. I just stared him down, chest rising and falling rapidly, thanks to my growing wrath.

"Fine." He sighed, the sound mixed with annoyance and frustration. "I accept."

Instead of letting go of him and expecting him to follow, I kept the tight hold on his shirt and dragged his tall ass around the table.

"Am I a dog you're trying to leash?" he asked as we got to the stairs.

"You're a big fucking pain in my ass," I said harshly.

He gasped dramatically, but I forced my eyes to keep looking toward the front door of the library that I intended to drag him out of.

"That's quite the colorful language, *Dawsyn*," he goaded, but I didn't bite. Not yet anyway.

I'd show him *colorful* as soon as I got him in the gym next door.

I was about to start and finish World War III, with Cillian as the only casualty.

Chapter Eighteen

CILLIAN

The one thing I was certain Dawsyn hadn't thought of when she decided to come kick my ass—or at least attempt to—was that the last time she used physical force against me, the cloak over my dragon energy broke.

Thankfully, I had anticipated more aggression coming my way from her, and I'd been doubling down on my shield. I was *mostly* certain the use of two dragon scales would keep her from outing me. I probably should have asked her to test that theory before she'd begun dragging me out of the library and there were dozens of eyes watching our every move. Too late for that now.

"You had no right to tell River what you did," she grumbled, not looking at me, and headed in the direction of the gym that was next to the library.

"I didn't realize you kept secrets from your best friend," I replied nonchalantly.

Her movements came to an abrupt stop, then she slowly turned around, eyes alight with unfiltered wrath and jaw locked tight. "I was keeping it for *you*, dick shit."

Dick shit? I hadn't heard that one before, not even over the last four weeks being at the academy.

"I didn't actually think you would." I shrugged. I'd certainly hoped she would and wouldn't lie to myself and say it didn't bring me at least an ounce of joy when I realized River had zero clue about my connection to Dawsyn.

She threw her arms halfway into the air, then pointed at the gym. "Inside. Now."

"Yes ma'am." I walked behind her stomping form with a grin on my face that further served to piss her off.

Dawsyn was an alpha, through and through. I could feel the power radiating off her when she was this upset. Its energy moved over me, testing my strengths, taunting my dragon to come forward and submit.

I should have probably been more careful with my words, but if this was the only way I could get physically close to her, I was going to take it.

She pushed open the main door to the gym, the sound echoing across the open building. I'd yet to come in here because I had no desire to be challenged by any of the other students.

My eyes glanced around, finding a boxing ring in one corner, weightlifting equipment opposite to that, and blue padded mats covering the floor on the other half of the spacious room. There were a few doors on the left wall that I assumed led to bathrooms and showers or housed more equipment.

"Move," Dawsyn snarled to those few still on the mats. Her voice rumbled with tantalizing alpha energy that drew me closer to her.

When she turned around, she had to look up sharply in order to see my face. "We're going to fight, and when you lose, you're going to kiss my toes in front of everyone that's come to watch you fall from that shit-covered pedestal you seem to think you belong on."

I smirked and tilted my head closer to her face. "And what if I win? What are you going to do for me?"

The right side of her mouth curved up, and her eyes sparked with deviousness. "I'll let you live."

I barked out a laugh, but she didn't return the gesture, which sobered me rather quickly. My hand moved between our close forms. "You have a deal, *Dawsyn*."

I drew her name out, enunciating the "syn" with a low rumble in my voice. I wasn't an idiot. I wasn't going to forget how she'd reacted earlier. I'd seen and even sensed how she responded to it that morning. Cheeks stained crimson, her chest filling from her increased breaths. Sure, she'd acted annoyed, but that was only because her name falling from my lips made her *feel*. That was something she couldn't hide from me, no matter how much she wished she could.

There was a flush to her cheeks as her glare intensified. "Deal."

Our hands shook, and I was equally pleased and disappointed when her tightened grip didn't elicit even the faintest of sparks between us.

Before she released my hand, she took the opportunity to shove me back. I stumbled from the unexpected force but didn't fall on my ass.

Her head shook and she tsked with her smirk back in

place. "Always be prepared, Cillian. Didn't your parents teach you that?"

"They did. They also taught me not to play with my prey," I quipped just as I swung my foot out, knocking her legs out from underneath her.

The indignation on her face was almost laughable, but I didn't think it would help keep all my body parts intact if I chose to grin in her direction.

She was back up on her feet in under two seconds. When I expected her to swing at me, she backed up, drawing me forward.

Normally, when I was challenged by someone like this, I had at least seen them fight before or knew where they had received their training from. With Dawsyn, I knew nothing about her style or what standards she held herself to, but I was eager to find out. Even if I ended up with a few bruises.

A crowd grew around us, but everyone stayed quiet outside of a few hushed murmurs wondering who we were and why we were fighting.

"She's the founder's daughter," I heard someone whisper, but I didn't get to hear anything else before Dawsyn attacked.

She went low, using one arm to wrap up my thighs and the other to punch me in the kidney. The hard impact vibrated straight through my ribs, making me wince.

I growled, barely catching myself with my right hand and blocking her follow-up hits with the left. She crawled on top of me, attempting to pin my arms to my sides, but while she was quicker than I expected, I still packed twice as much muscle than my mate could ever dream of having on her delectable body.

My hips bucked up, tossing her to the side while my hand itched to hold her against me. I reached for her to pin her down like she had me, but again, her speed bested me.

Dawsyn was on two feet again. I half expected her to shift, but at least she was being fair in knowing that shifting wasn't possible for me.

"How are the ribs feeling?" she taunted.

I didn't bother to respond. Talking during battle was never a favorite of mine. Sure, it could distract my opponent, but it could also take away from where my focus should be, which currently needed to be on getting Dawsyn on her back.

The she-wolf was too fast on her feet.

I feigned right, then went left, wrapping my arms around her upper body and using my weight to force us both to the ground.

Only my need to protect her lessened the effectiveness of my move. At the last second, my hand shot out and stopped me from using my full size against her.

I couldn't, nor did I want to, hurt my mate. Even if that meant kissing her toes.

I'd known telling River would get me in trouble, and I had hoped doing so would be worth every ounce of fury I'd made Dawsyn feel.

As I pressed the full length of my body over hers, trapping her against the ground, I knew right then it was absolutely worth it.

With every wicked punch she threw my way and connected, I felt a surge between our bond. It wasn't like the initial time when she shoved me, but there was something there that I craved.

A longing to be closer to her even when she thought she hated me.

A need to hold her tighter even when I knew she struggled to get free.

A demand to claim her even when I knew I had no right to.

Knowing there was no possible way I could hurt Dawsyn enough to win, I defended myself for a solid five minutes, then I slowed my movements.

She landed leg kicks to my thighs and ribs. She punched my body anywhere she could reach, her grunts growing louder as the seconds ticked by. It wasn't until her breathing began to calm that I finally let her put me on my back again.

"Let" wasn't exactly right, though. My mate was strong. She could have likely held her own in a fair fight, but since I wasn't willing to drag this out for the hours it might have lasted otherwise, I did what I knew I was going to from the very beginning.

I let Dawsyn pin me to the ground.

Her legs tightened around my body, her hips hovering just over mine as she used the weight of her body to push her forearm into my neck. The position made it hard to breathe, but not impossible. I could have stayed this way for the rest of the day. When her eyes met mine, filled with hunger, I knew I'd made the right choice giving up.

Her gaze burned into me, and I raised my head higher. My tongue darted out, licking my lips, and she moved her stare to watch the quick action just as I hoped. Her chest filled with air, and the tension on my neck eased ever so slightly.

Our mouths were inches apart. All I had to do was lift

myself just a bit further up, but I didn't want our first kiss to be out of passionate rage. I wanted the hunger in her eyes to fill the rest of her body so immensely that she couldn't stand the thought of there being any space between us.

Plus, knowing that we had a crowd watching, I forcefully dropped my head back to the mat and tapped my fingers against the side of her leg where my hand was still pinned.

"Are you giving up?" she heaved, her words no longer laced with their early venom.

"You win, Dawsyn." I kept her gaze for as long as she would let me, forcing my body to relax and convince her that I wasn't trying to play any tricks.

She pulled the rest of the pressure from my throat, fisted her hands, then punched my chest with both of them. "Stay there so you can follow through on your end of the deal."

There was a hint of a smile on her lips, but it was gone before anyone other than me could see.

She turned to the horde of people and threw her arms in the air with a triumphant grin. People cheered, mostly the women that I'd ignored over the last several weeks. Men merely shook their heads, likely understanding the position I'd been in.

As I got to my knees, I reached for Dawsyn's foot, but she stepped back. "Oh no," she tittered. "I said you have to kiss my *toes*. Not my shoe."

She couldn't be fucking serious.

The longer I stared up at her mischievous eyes, the better I knew she wasn't going to let up on this. She kicked one Converse off, then reached down to pull off her undoubtedly sweaty sock.

Her toes wiggled over the mat, and she stepped closer. "Pucker up, buttercup."

If I was going to have to go through this sort of... torture, then I was going to make her feel every bit as uncomfortable as I was.

Inching closer, I sat on my knees and leaned forward. I wrapped one hand lightly around her ankle before letting it slide further up, squeezing her calf. Her heartbeat increased, and I lowered my head, smirking as I used my other hand to firmly hold the base of her foot, almost to the point of massaging it.

Tension radiated from her body while the crowd watching stopped talking shit about me, instead zeroing in on the fact that I might have been ready to kiss Dawsyn's toes, but she wasn't getting the last laugh.

The pad of my thumb rubbed over the arch of her foot, garnering a flinch from her that slithered through her entire body.

"Just do it already," she hissed.

"As you wish," I said with a deep tenor.

My head moved closer so that I didn't knock her off balance by lifting her leg too much. My lips pressed over her big toe first, then the next before I glanced up at her. "You did say kiss your *toes*, right?"

Before she could jerk out of my hold, I pecked at two more. I might have had bruises growing on my ribs, but my chest was full, as if I'd been the winner and not Dawsyn.

She hastily grabbed her sock and shoe, then poked a finger in my shoulder. "This isn't over."

"Far from it, sweetheart," I answered softly, but with a grin still plastered to my face as I got up from the floor.

The harumph that left her only made me smile wider. At least, until I saw the crowd still waiting. I dropped the happy look and growled. "Show's over."

A few of them let out sighs of disappointment, but they all began to disperse.

By the time I made it outside where I knew Dawsyn had run to, she was nowhere to be seen. I thought to go after her, but she likely needed to cool down for multiple reasons. Plus, I had a library to get back to and answers to find.

I also had more motivation than ever before to figure out a solution for my realm, because something told me that once that was off my shoulders, Dawsyn wasn't going to be able to run very far from me.

Chapter Nineteen

DAWSYN

One minute, that had gone exactly as I'd hoped, then the next...it was a damned disaster. Cillian was more cunning than I'd given him credit for. I couldn't forget that in the future.

For a brief moment, I'd thought he was going to kiss me. Worse, I hadn't even considered trying to stop him. I'd been imagining the feel of his lips on mine for so many days now that finally knowing was worth whatever the kiss would have cost me.

And the way he'd held my foot, then slipped his hand beneath my jeans to cup my calf, was shockingly powerful. The bond surged through my leg, up my stomach, and straight to my chest before blossoming through the rest of my body. Even with a crowd watching, I'd wanted him to stay there forever, right at my feet.

He let you win, my wolf said with a haughtiness I didn't appreciate, especially since she'd been ignoring me.

Now, I was going to do the same to her.

After I put my shoe back on, I was tempted to shift, but

my wolf didn't deserve that kind of control at the moment, so instead, I started to jog, then run, back to Baker House.

I wasn't sure if Cillian would follow me, but I wasn't in the right headspace to face him. Hell, I wasn't in the mood to face River, either, after the things he'd said, but I didn't know where else to go.

Except, when I got back to the room, his books were gone and the dorm was empty.

Small favors.

I went to my room, grabbed the bag I'd made with all my bathroom stuff, and headed to the communal showers.

The need to wash Cillian's touch off my body warred inside me. On one hand, I felt calmer than I had in days. On the other, I was incredibly frustrated *because* of that fact and my earlier revelations about already knowing I didn't actually want to reject Cillian... But what Brixley had told me still heavily weighed on my mind.

I was a mess.

Physically and emotionally. So, a shower it was.

You should have talked to him after the fight was over, my wolf said when I walked into the bathroom.

I grumbled loudly as I entered the shower stall. With too much force, I jerked the water handle back, bending the metal.

Damn it, I needed to get a hold of myself.

You don't get to choose when or when not to speak to me, I snarled at my wolf. *I needed you, and you disappeared just because we didn't agree. That's a level of bullshit I don't need right now.*

She was quiet for a moment while I waited for the water to warm up. I undressed in the corner of the stall where the shower spray didn't quite reach and next to the shelf where I set my bag.

By the time I was under the steaming spray of water, I was no less tense, even though my wolf was back to talking to me.

I'm not used to us disagreeing on such an important matter, she said. *But I'm glad you see that rejecting him isn't the right choice.*

That's not exactly where I'm at with this whole thing, I replied. *You heard Brixley.*

What she'd sensed about me completing the mate bond with someone I chose and not a fated match... I couldn't ignore that.

Visions are often misinterpreted, she countered. *You'd really throw away a fated mate bond because of one?*

No, I wouldn't. At least not for that particular reason alone. *But even if I did ignore what Brixley told me, what about the logistics and my family, our pack? Can't you understand how hard of a decision this is, even if I don't want* to reject him? *That doesn't mean I won't have to.*

As I finished washing my hair, then began scrubbing at my body, she finally replied, *I understand. It just doesn't feel right.*

In that, we could agree. None of this felt right. Coming to this school. Meeting Cillian. Learning dragons existed. Not wanting him even when I knew he made my body feel like a live wire with just a single touch.

We'll figure it out eventually, I said. *Just don't disappear on me again.*

I won't. I'm sorry.

I'm sorry, too.

And just like that, at least one part of my life was back to normal. Now, if only I could live each day merely thankful for small favors, there was a chance I might just survive this shit show.

TWO DAYS LATER, THOSE COUPLE OF SMALL favors I'd been eternally grateful for were nowhere to be seen.

River hadn't come back to the dorm. At least not while I was camped out, waiting for him. I only left a couple of times, once to shower and a couple more outings to get food. I had no idea where he was staying. Justine claimed she didn't know, either, when she'd come by to gossip about my public fight with Cillian.

Apparently, the school was abuzz with interest, wondering if we really hated each other or if there was something more, like they'd suspected before.

My phone rang on the cushion next to me where I was sitting on the couch. I scrambled for it, hoping River was finally calling me back, but before I could be careful with my fingers, I was answering a call from my parents. Not my best friend.

"Hey," I said awkwardly.

"Hey?" Dad grumbled. "It's been over a week since you've answered one of my calls and all I get is 'hey'?"

I winced. Yes, I was an adult, and yes, they drove me crazy some days, but we were a close family. Just because I didn't want to settle for the pack life just yet didn't mean I didn't appreciate the life I'd had there.

"Hello, Dad," I said with more excitement. "How are you? I've missed you terribly and it's so good to hear your voice."

"Don't placate me, child," he said, but there was a slight chuckle to his tone.

"How are you?" Mom asked next, but the tension in her voice made me give pause.

They knew something, and I was two seconds from being backed into a corner if I didn't answer correctly. I'd learned that lesson many times as a child, which I no longer was, but damn if my parents didn't still hold a power over me even as an adult.

I quickly began to wonder about the things they could know. Had Brixley outed me? No, if they knew I was possibly mated, they'd be here in person.

Were they upset I hadn't enrolled in classes yet? Possibly. I'd start there.

"Good," I answered. "I've been visiting some of the classes, trying to see what might interest me before spring semester closes for enrollment."

"Is that so?" Dad questioned. "Anything else? Find any recreational activities that have piqued your interest?"

That corner was getting closer and closer.

"Not really, but I've made some new friends," I said, then tried to tell them about Justine, but was quickly interrupted.

"Not even training in the gym?" he pushed.

Shit.

They knew about my fight with Cillian.

Of course they knew. Half of the teachers were

acquaintances of theirs, ones who wouldn't mind getting in good with the strongest wolf pack in the United States.

"I wouldn't call what I did an interest in gym," I said without an ounce of shame.

"Then, what would you call picking a fight with one of the hybrid students?" he chastised.

I took a calming breath. He was talking to me as if I was a troubled teen. I wasn't going to give him any joy out of thinking he was right by acting like one.

"I would call it handling my own business," I replied, my voice even. "He said something to River that he shouldn't have, and he's not exactly the nicest person to the other students. Someone needed to put him in his place and that someone happened to be me."

"Did it now?" my dad pressed.

"Did it have to be you and Mom to change the supernatural world?" I countered. "Sometimes these things just fall into our laps."

I could hear the smile in Mom's voice as she responded. "Well, then we're proud of you for handling things however they needed to be handled. You're okay, though?"

"Of course," I answered. "He never stood a chance."

That might have been stretching the truth, given his genetics, but they didn't need to know that.

Dad stayed quiet, but Mom continued, "You mentioned some friends earlier. Anyone we know?"

Gods, I hoped not. I didn't need them trying to intervene more than I already assumed they were. Shaking them even at twenty-two was harder than I liked.

"A vampire named Just—" A knock at my door cut me off. "Hold on a second."

I got off the couch and put the phone on mute as I answered the door. Justine was on the other side, grinning and reaching for my hand. "Come on. River is back."

"Back?" I asked. "What do you mean *back*?"

"We couldn't find him because he wasn't here," she answered. "He's in class now, but if you hurry, you can stop him as he leaves the room."

I couldn't believe he'd left the campus and didn't tell me. That hurt almost more than how he'd spoken to me before.

Remembering my parents were still on the line, I unmuted them and apologized. "I need to go. The friend I was just going to tell you about—Justine—she's here and she needs my help with something."

"Hi, Dawsyn's mom and dad!" she called out.

"Alright, honey," Mom said. "Have fun and please don't wait so long to check in next time."

"Yeah, sure. Love you both."

"We love you too, Dawsyn," Dad said, then the call ended.

I wasn't sure that went how they were hoping, but at least they didn't know I was mated or that Cillian was a dragon shifter, not the hybrid everyone else assumed.

"Hurry," Justine said, already walking away from my door. "He's all the way in Dragontail Hall."

This state had some weird-ass names for their mountains and rivers. I still didn't understand why the academy used them to name their buildings, but this particular choice was an incredible coincidence of a name. Hopefully.

Justine kept a fast pace once we got outside. Not quite running, but definitely not walking.

"His class is out in one minute, and then he's free the rest of the day," she said. "You'll have to track him if you don't catch him now."

Not that I couldn't do that. Well, most of the time. I just didn't want to be that forceful in my attempts to get River to talk to me. He was my best friend. I hated this tension between us, but I knew him well enough that he would only talk to me when he was ready.

Though, that didn't mean I couldn't show him that I missed him in the meantime, while hoping he wouldn't shun me the first second that he saw me.

We went behind the main admin building, cut through the common area, bypassing the library and gym before finally reaching Dragontail.

"Right there." Justine pointed to a still-closed door. "I'm going to go before he's mad at both of us. I didn't tell you anything."

Without thinking, I pulled her into a quick hug. "Thank you."

She wrapped her arms around me and laughed. "No problem."

The vampire sped off just as the class door opened. I moved to the side and watched students file out of the room until River finally came into appearance.

His head was down, auburn hair falling over his forehead and books in hand. Just as I reached out to touch him, his head snapped up and hazel eyes widened at me.

"What are you doing here?" he asked with more tension than I was hoping for.

"Looking for my best friend," I said with a shrug. "Have you seen him?"

He rolled his eyes. "Nope." Then he brushed by me.

"Are you going to talk to me?"

He scoffed. "You were the one who said we needed some time apart."

"To cool down, not to ignore each other for days," I said, trying and failing not to get frustrated with him.

His hard eyes cut back to me. "Maybe I haven't cooled down yet. This wasn't something little, D. It was big. Really fucking big, and you didn't trust me with it. Makes me wonder what else you haven't told me."

Mother shit shittery.

If I didn't come clean about dragon shifters now, I wasn't sure he'd ever forgive me when he found out later.

But...Cillian.

He'd shared what I considered to be *my* secret, but did that make it right for me to share his?

River was my best friend. I knew we could trust him just like we could Brixley, but this wasn't the place for us to have this conversation.

"Your hesitation is all the answer I need," he snapped before I could relay my thoughts. "Don't follow me."

"River, wait," I pleaded. "I can explain."

He spun back around and towered over me. "But will you, Dawsyn? Because something tells me that you certainly *can*. Yet, you still haven't."

Just when I thought my anger at Cillian had subsided, I was quickly proven wrong. I hated that I'd been put in this position to choose between honoring my best friend and the promise I made Cillian. If this affected just him, I wanted to believe I wouldn't hesitate so much, but there was a whole realm that was already dying.

I couldn't just blurt out what I knew in the middle of the hallway, but that was exactly what River expected of me.

"Just as I thought," he said with a harsh shake of his head. "I'll see you around, Dawsyn."

Damn everything all to hell. What was I supposed to do now?

Chapter Twenty

CILLIAN

There were more books on vampires than I expected there to be. Annoyingly so. My only saving grace was that I could check them out and take them back to my room. Though, that wasn't the only place I did research.

It had been three days since I last saw Dawsyn in the gym. I knew that the last time we were apart for too long, she'd gotten sick. I didn't want that for her, so I did—and was currently doing—the only pathetic thing I could think of.

At night, when I was hopeful that she and River would be asleep, I snuck out and sat next to their door. The idea was that my close proximity would prevent her from feeling miserable, but since I hadn't seen her leave the dorm, I had no way to be sure it was working.

Hell, I hadn't even seen River, but he could be avoiding me as well. Who knew what he and Dawsyn had talked about after he let her know that I'd said she was my mate.

She could have told him I was a dragon shifter. Honestly, I wouldn't be surprised and wouldn't even be mad. Dawsyn owed me nothing. Even though she'd been pissed off during most of our interactions, I wanted her to be happy.

Closing another book with information I didn't really need to know, I picked up the third one of the night.

My eyes were burning, and I was yawning every five minutes, but my time here was running out. Not only with Dawsyn, but for my realm. I was supposed to head home in just one week.

Nannio was back to ignoring me, and if it wasn't for Dawsyn, I'd have stormed back into Drago days ago.

It was as if my crazy grandmother knew what I would find here and used that to keep me away. I just didn't understand why. I wasn't a child. I'd trained to fight against those who wished us harm. I had my lightning energy that badly needed to be released and could possibly help thwart off the worst of whatever they were experiencing.

So many questions and not enough damn answers.

I threw the book open with more force than necessary and winced when I heard the spine crack. These weren't new books, so I needed to be more careful. Otherwise, I had a feeling I was going to be cut off.

The librarian was already side-eyeing me, and I didn't like it.

With more words blending together as the night got later, I was two seconds from getting up and going to get some rest when a familiar face was coming down the hallway.

The same black-rimmed glasses guy I'd seen in the library before was in our dorm building, and he was holding a book in his hands, clutched to his chest.

He pushed his glasses up and stopped next to me. "Cillian?"

"What do you want?" I deadpanned. I didn't even have the energy to be curious or annoyed.

"Why are you reading books about vampires?" he asked.

Since he didn't want to answer me, there wasn't a chance in hell that I was going to answer him.

I got off the floor before we woke up Dawsyn or River and picked up the books that I had with me. I tried to walk past the hybrid, but he stepped in my path.

"I think I can help you," he said, looking up at me.

By supernatural standards, he was short. I had at least six inches on him and probably fifty pounds of muscle, but he didn't seem the least bit intimidated by me as I stared down at him. I probably had death in my eyes, because that was how I felt.

"No," I said, then brushed past him. He grabbed my arm, and I turned back with a raised brow. "You might want to rethink your actions."

My warning was clear and delivered with a rumble in my chest, but still, he wasn't afraid.

He waved the book he'd brought with him in the air. "You need this."

"How the fuck do you know what I need?" I snapped, no longer too tired to react.

Removing his hand from my arm, he glanced around us, but it wasn't necessary. We were the only idiots up at three in the morning. "I just do. Call it intuition if you will."

"Intuition?" That wasn't the answer I expected, and it

infuriated me more than I should have let it. "How about I call it bullshit? How did you know I need that book?"

He held the book against his chest again. "You can choose to think whatever you want, but I'm not lying. I have no reason to." He glanced around again, lowering his voice. "You're different from the other hybrids like me, and you spend a lot of time questioning people or in the library. If you didn't think others were noticing, you were wrong. I even heard two of the professors talking about you. One I didn't know. The other was Professor Hayes."

That motherfucker.

He was the one who told me to search the library for vampire books.

"What's that book about?" I asked since I couldn't see the cover.

"The original witch families," he answered, his knuckles turning white from holding the damn thing so tightly.

That was what I'd thought I needed before I so stupidly and easily believed Professor Hayes. A fact that had my chest heaving with fury.

Before I began raging or trying to bargain for a book I may or may not have needed, I had more questions to ask, so that I didn't fuck up again. "So, your intuition led you to overhearing Professor Hayes tell someone this was the book I specifically needed?"

He shook his head. "Well, sort of. I take one of his history classes. I overheard the conversation thanks to dumb luck, but he hadn't said which book you were looking for. When I snuck into his office, this was the only one locked up."

"Locked up? And you just so happened to break it

free?" I asked, giving him another onceover. He maybe weighed one-hundred-sixty pounds with very little muscle. Didn't seem likely that he used brute force.

"I didn't *break* anything," he corrected. "I found the key to the locked drawer thanks to my intuition that told me Professor Hayes believes that he's untouchable. Why not leave the key taped to the underside of his chair?"

I nodded toward the book. "What do you want in exchange for it?"

While I had no proof that I needed what the guy had found, if it wasn't going to cost me much to have it, why not check things out?

He flinched back and widened his eyes. "I don't want anything."

It was taking more effort than I had the energy for to keep my growing ire over this whole situation at bay, but I still tried since none of it was directed at the guy in front of me. At least not yet.

That damned professor on the other hand... I would have to do something about him, but I was more furious that he'd lied directly to my face, and I believed him.

I'd been too damned desperate for answers, which caused me to make a mistake, but that was going to stop now.

"What's your name?" I asked.

"Brace Samson," he answered.

I gave him another onceover. "Well, Brace Samson. If you don't need or want anything, are you going to give me that book you're holding so tightly to?"

He glanced down, gazing at the smooth black leather. "You're not going to hurt anyone with this, right?"

I leaned closer and looked him dead in the eyes. "What's that intuition of yours telling you now?"

He swallowed thickly. "To give you the book and run."

"Yet, you're still here, making sure you're not putting important information into the wrong hands." Maybe Brace could be useful. He wasn't strong, but he was smart and brave. Those two things weren't always easy to find in a person.

"Like I said before, you're different," he replied. "I don't know why, but you're not like me or the other witch-wolf hybrids."

He had no idea how right he was about that, but I was done with this conversation before his so-called intuition led him down a path that we couldn't come back from.

"I'm not going to hurt anyone," I said. "I promise. In fact, I hope to save some people."

"Okay." He handed the book right over. "I hope you find what you need then."

"Just like that you're going to give it to me?"

He grinned and pushed his glasses up again. "I wasn't telling the truth before. I don't have intuition. But I can tell if someone is lying. You're not what you say, but you do want to help people. I'm okay with not knowing anything else. In fact, I'd prefer it." He turned away and waved with his back to me. "Goodnight, Cillian."

What the fuck had just happened?

I held the book in my hands as I watched him go up the stairs, assumingly to his dorm. I didn't like how easy that was, and trusting he wouldn't tell anyone what he thought or had learned during this little encounter was risky, but at this point, I didn't have any other choice.

In fact, at the moment, all I had was a book about witches that was pulsing with original energy and should have been locked up somewhere safer than that dumbass professor's desk.

It seemed as if I wasn't going to be getting the rest that I thought I was. I had a book to read and a solution to find for at least one of my problems.

Chapter Twenty-One

DAWSYN

I'd wanted Mystics Academy to be the first stay on my road to experiencing freedom for three reasons: I wanted to spend more time with River, I could meet new people easier, and I was rather sure that I wouldn't catch any hell for coming here.

Given the last one was the only one I hadn't been certain about, yet the only one that had come to fruition, I was becoming a grouchy bitch.

River still never came home, and I didn't want to leave my dorm to meet new people because I had a feeling that if I walked out that door, River would either come waltzing in and I'd miss him or I'd run right into Cillian.

I wasn't as irritated at him as I was before, but I was... something. I had no proper words for my feelings. Everything inside me was warring, and it was annoying as shit.

It's only annoying *because you're avoiding everything*, my wolf said.

I scoffed. *No, I'm waiting for River. The one person I want to talk to.*

You talked to him before. By leaving the dorm.

She was right, but stalking his classes didn't seem like the best way to earn his forgiveness.

Telling him about Cillian would solve that, she reminded me.

I know that, which is why I intend on telling him as soon as we're alone. I can't just blurt out that dragon shifters are real in public. Cillian would lose his mind.

Hmm, seems interesting that you'd rather catch hell from River than our mate.

My chest rumbled. I wasn't going to confirm her statement by replying.

Stupid me for missing that damn wolf while she'd been ignoring me. I nearly told her to go away, but—like it or not—she was sort of all I had at the moment.

At least until my nose twitched and Cillian's earthy scent burned through me.

My chest expanded, and I took a deep breath, glaring at the door that I was certain he stood behind.

Maybe I was still more furious with him than I'd told myself. I was at least *something* with him.

I stayed frozen on the couch with the book I'd been reading—or at least attempting to read—in hand.

No noise came from the hallway, but I could still smell him, then wondered if he knew I was in here. Did I really care? I wanted the answer to be no, but that was part of the reason I felt so ragey.

I didn't want to care or be attracted to his five o'clock shadow or the way he enunciated my name. Or the way the heat from his body seared into my skin, making my body want him when my mind didn't.

I never asked for any of it. In fact, I'd begged for the complete opposite, and yet... The universe had basically given the middle finger to my wants.

But had it? my wolf challenged. *Deep down, do you really want to be alone? You keep saying you want freedom and I understand not living in your parents' shadow, but freedom doesn't mean you can't have a mate. He may want the same things as you, but you haven't given him the chance to show you that.*

Closing my eyes, I tried to see her point. I imagined not being so furious with Cillian. Not hating the idea of a mate. Instead, I pictured our situation now, just a little different.

Cillian still needed to save his realm. He could do that, and then maybe he'd want to come back here. Maybe he could find a way to blend in with our world more permanently.

If I didn't focus so much on not wanting to be tied down, I could—in theory—picture a scenario where we both got what we wanted.

My body shuddered, but it wasn't from repulsion.

What I was seeing, what I could tangibly feel as a possible future, it felt fucking amazing. Like the puzzle pieces that had been raining down on me these last couple of weeks were finally finding their home.

There was still one black cloud in that picture, no matter which way I looked at it. I was going to have a chosen mate in my life. I didn't know when or how or why, but I trusted Brixley's vision, even if my wolf didn't.

That was enough to stop me from opening the door to my dorm and throwing myself at Cillian.

Maybe the chosen mate Brixley sensed was you finally choosing Cillian, my wolf added to my lingering thoughts, while I listened for sounds coming from the shifter in question, still standing at my door.

Part of me wondered if my wolf was right. After wanting to reject him so thoroughly, could my choice not to do so be what Brixley was picturing? It was possible, but I was out of time to consider that at the moment.

Cillian's voice pulled me out of the insanity. "Dawsyn?"

Gods, it wasn't fair the amount of power he had over me when he said my name. The way he spoke it with such reverence, drawing out each syllable... It sent shivers throughout my body each and every damned time.

I got up from the couch and set the book I couldn't even remember the title of on the table, then went to the door. Before opening it, I smoothed my hands over my wrinkled t-shirt and hair. I was a bit of a mess, but at least there weren't any stains on my jeans.

My fingers curled around the doorknob, twisted, and pulled it toward me. I stepped back and steadied myself just before I looked up at his face.

Damn him. He was still just as lickable as he was three days ago.

Huh. I just realized we'd been apart all this time and I didn't get sick once. Not like before.

I wasn't sure if that was because I wasn't mentally trying to reject the idea of our bond every five minutes or something else. It was the *something else* that frightened me.

"Are you okay?" he asked, staring intently at me.

"Yeah." I stepped further to the side. "I'm assuming you want to come in?"

He held a newer book in his hands and handed it to me. "I found something. I can't get a hold of my grandmother or uncle, and I was hoping the urge you had to kick my ass had lessened enough that you could look at it with me."

My eyes stared at his face as he spoke. Not at the book that could hold the answers to send him back where he came from, but at his face that was the least guarded I'd ever seen it.

His eyes were bloodshot, likely from lack of sleep, considering what he had between his fingers. His cheeks seemed shallow, and his clothes were twice as wrinkled as mine, but that wasn't what got to me most.

It was the way he wouldn't quite look me in the eyes and the way he rolled his lower lip between his teeth and tapped his fingers over the black leather cover.

He was nervous or uncertain, and he'd still come to me. If he had his answer, he could have run home, especially after not being able to get a hold of his family.

Yet, here he was. Standing before me, knowing there was a good chance that I'd slam the door in his face.

I expected my wolf to smart off with something that was supposed to make me feel something positive toward the dragon, but she'd stayed silent. Surprisingly, I didn't need her snark to sway my feelings one way or the other.

The image I'd been conjuring before opening the door, the one that showed a future with me and Cillian finding a way to work through our obstacles... Those puzzle pieces stitched tighter together, solidifying until there were no lines between the pieces and no black cloud. Just us.

Seeing him before me, vulnerable and trusting me to help with something so important to him... That changed something in me.

An unknown chosen mate be damned. I was fucking tired of this fight. I couldn't do it anymore. Not when the euphoria I was imagining our future could be filled me so thoroughly.

There would be no more second-guessing. No more trying to choose between this or that. I was done telling him and the universe that I didn't want him anymore.

Did I want to jump him and complete the bond right here in the doorway? Hell, no. But I also didn't want to turn him away or punch him in the face any longer. Or merely help him just because that meant him going away.

No, I wanted to help because I...cared.

I welcomed Cillian inside, and he went straight to the small couch. Not the table where we would have had plenty of space between us. No, the couch where I'd have to lean into him to see what he'd found.

The annoyance I might have felt over that move before my change of heart never came. Not even as I sat down next to him, very aware of how his legs widened. How the warmth from his body seeped into mine, finding a home in my core and making me really damn uncomfortable.

The bond I had just decided to stop rejecting flared to life, still there and perfectly intact, regardless of my prolonged stubbornness.

The pulsing in my chest forced me to close my eyes briefly and take a few calming breaths. I needed to get my shit together.

Sure, I didn't want to cast him away, but jumping him seemed a bit of a dramatic change, even for fated mates.

Slow and steady. Very fucking slow.

That might drive others insane, but it was what I needed, no matter what my body was trying to say.

"What did you find?" I finally asked, quickly looking up at him and then down at the book.

There was a crease between his brows as if he had something to say unrelated to what he'd found, but mercifully, he kept whatever that was to himself.

His attention went back to the book. He flipped the pages to where there were tabs sticking out everywhere. When he stopped, there was a yellow sticky with an asterisk marked at the end. He turned the book in his lap so that I could see better.

"This is a book someone from one of the original witch families wrote," he said. "It doesn't say who the author is, but their use of 'we' is pretty common throughout some of these passages."

I tilted my head, taking in the book with its pristine cream-colored pages and smooth edges. "You mean someone descended from one of the original families?"

His head shook. "That's what I thought, too. I never would have picked this up, given how new it looks, but it seems to be magically protected. I couldn't even fold the pages when I found something I wanted to come back to. I had to use these tabs."

"And the author?" I asked.

"Like I said before, they use 'we' and don't talk about electricity or anything modern. And there's mention of the start of the Civil War," he said, his palm splayed over the pages. "This has to be an original member. Though, I can't tell from which family."

I knew someone who could, someone I'd trust with my life. But bringing my family into this—more than Brixley already was—wasn't something I was comfortable with. At least, not yet.

Cillian and I had a lot more to discuss before that happened. So, I kept that thought to myself and reached for the book. "Let me see."

Our fingers brushed together, a light—but noticeable—bolt of energy passing between us. Though, neither he nor I said anything.

He pointed to the middle of the right page. "I think this is talking about the spell I need to replicate, but it doesn't tell me everything I need to know."

The Surge

The Howe family took things too far this week. We were hoping to remain cordial with them, but alas, we had to eviscerate them. Jezebel tried to abduct Beatrix from our coven. The little witch might only be six years of age, but she proved to be even more powerful than we assumed and saved herself. Though, the strength that saved her is the very reason she was targeted.

Still, we had to retaliate. The Howes, and

any others who thought to come for one of our coven members, needed to understand that our family was not to be trifled with and after weeks of them attempting to siphon our powers, enough was enough.

Together, with myself, Jane, and Emma, we attacked. With the items we gathered and our combined energy, we were able to force enough magic on them that their energy surged, ceasing to aid in their defense.

In those brief moments of weakness, we struck them down. It was painful to end them so swiftly, but it was done with mercy and that was important to me.

Beatrix will be safe to grow into the powerful sorceress we suspect she will be and the rest of our coven will be protected from the attacks they have become accustomed to. At least for the time being.

The passage ended, and the remainder of the page was a drawing of several objects. One of which I'd seen, and hell, I was pretty sure I'd held it.

GiGi's silver chalice. It was engraved with the same three interconnected loops and something I'd attempted to drink apple juice from when I was young.

She'd never yelled so loud before, and I'd never again

touched her precious cup. But more importantly, I was rather certain that my GiGi was the Beatrix mentioned in the book.

"What is it?" Cillian asked, his eyes burning into me with optimism that I hoped I wasn't about to dash.

"I think I know this Beatrix," I said, "but if you want me to ask for her help, I won't lie to her. She's going to know your realm exists and even then, she might not help."

He flinched back, annoyance creasing his face. "Why wouldn't she help?"

I chuckled. "You'd need to have met my GiGi to understand the complexity of that answer. She has a big heart, but the attitude of... Well, just picture the most stubborn and obnoxious person you've ever met and times that by ten, then you have Beatrix."

"You called her GiGi." His brow furrowed. "Who is she to you?"

"Beatrix Jacobs is my grandmother for all intents and purposes," I said. "More importantly, she's the most powerful witch in existence. At least, she still claims to be. Nobody has dared to challenge her, even in her old age."

"If there's a chance that she can save my realm, then we need to tell her whatever she wants to know," he said, fingers tightly gripping the book still between us.

I hesitated, because while I really did want to help Cillian, there was something else I had to do.

"I need to tell River first," I said. "He's not speaking to me, because I wouldn't tell him what else I'd been keeping from him."

His hand reached for me, and I didn't flinch away when his warm fingers wrapped around mine. "I honestly expected you to tell him as soon as I accidentally told him that I was your mate. I didn't intend to cause problems for you, Dawsyn. I know we didn't start off in the best of ways, but I don't want you to be miserable. I trust you to tell whoever you believe you can trust and has a reason to know."

Mother shittery shit. That did things to my chest that I'd been badly trying to ignore since he walked into my dorm.

"Thank you," I said, squeezing his hand back that was still firmly holding on to me.

His other hand lifted and lightly brushed under my chin. "Thank you for not slamming the door in my face."

Dead. I was officially dead, and not one part of me could be mad about it anymore.

Chapter Twenty-Two

CILLIAN

Reaching out and touching Dawsyn hadn't been planned. Except when I did, I never wanted to stop. Something was different with her this morning. Maybe it was because I couldn't remember the last time I'd slept properly or what, but she wasn't pulling away from me like she had been in all our previous interactions.

My fingers brushed underneath her jaw, and the shiver that traveled through her body had my dragon rising to the surface.

I braced myself, keeping him down and staring into her golden eyes. "Dawsyn," I whispered.

"Hmmm," she replied, leaning into my touch.

Damn it. Never before had I wanted to kiss someone so badly, but it wasn't as if my mate had been consistent with her emotions toward me. One wrong move and I would be back to having her hate me.

That wasn't something I wanted to risk. Yet, as I continued to stare at her face, the bond between us thrumming to the beat of my increasing heart rate, my body inched forward, and her eyes watched my every movement.

She didn't push away. In fact, her gaze flicked down to my mouth and her tongue darted out lightly before she looked back up at my eyes.

"I don't think..." she trailed off, leaving me hanging.

I never had any clue what exactly this woman was thinking, and now was no different. It was maddening.

The hand that was still holding hers moved, and I wrapped my fingers behind her neck. "You don't think what?"

My words were soft yet pleading for her to put me out of misery.

I needed her to tell me she'd been wrong before. That regardless of all the obstacles I knew we faced, we'd somehow figure this out. That fate couldn't be wrong. Dawsyn was meant to be mine.

"I'm thinking I've lost my mind," she replied quietly, briefly slicing my heart in two, "but I can't find a reason to care anymore."

She leaned forward, rapidly closing the distance between us.

My fingers splayed around her neck while my other hand tangled in her hair. Her lips pressed against mine, soft at first, then demanding. I kissed her back, reminding myself not to devour her until she made it clear that this was what she wanted. That fighting the bond was what she couldn't care about any longer.

Her hands reached up and grabbed my shirt, using the tight grip to lift herself up and closer. She was practically on her knees next to me when she deepened the kiss, pushing me back against the cushions.

I opened my mouth to her, our tongues greeting each other like old lovers, eager to caress the other.

She pushed against my shoulders, guiding my body to the side until my head was on the arm of the couch. She straddled my waist with her legs, and her hands pressed over my chest as she grinned above me. "Too much?"

I gripped her hips and shook my head. "Never too much when it comes to you, Dawsyn."

Her teeth scraped over her lower lip. "It should be too much. I told you that I wanted to reject you. You should hate me."

"I could never hate you." Not even if she had found a way to break our bond. "You can reject me again tomorrow and every day after that and I'm not going anywhere. I might have to help my realm, but you're just as important to me."

Hell, she could probably ask me to choose between her and them. At this point, I would pick her every single time. Thankfully, something told me that Dawsyn valued the lives of others more than she was willing to be selfish, which made me want her even more.

"We have a lot of things standing in the way of us being together," she said, her thighs tightening against my sides and positioning herself over my hardening cock before continuing. "Dying realms, hidden dragons, logistics…just to name a few."

I groaned, but not because of all she'd listed. My fingers pushed into her jeans, squeezing her hips and the edge of her ass.

"I hear you, but is that really what you want to worry about right now?" My hands moved from her hips, up her sides, and stopped with my thumbs right beneath the curve of her breasts.

She shook her head, leaning down closer to me, and lowering her voice. "I don't want to think about anything right now. Consequences be damned."

Her lips quickly found their way back to mine, our mouths clashing together once more as our hands moved in frenzied motions over each other's bodies.

My heart was trying to burst from my chest—or maybe that was just our connection—and scales peeked out through my skin, making dark outlines on my exposed arms and hands. I was losing control with her, but I didn't care.

I needed to taste her and feel her body against mine more than I'd needed anything ever before.

How I could have thought for one second that walking away from her was the right thing to do was beyond me.

"Cillian," she murmured against my lips.

One of my hands slipped over her ass, holding her against my growing erection as she ground over me. "I'm right here and I'm not going anywhere."

I kissed her again, angling her head and deepening the kiss until I couldn't tell where her mouth began and mine ended. Her moans were slowly killing me, but I was following her direction, and until she started to remove clothes, I managed to keep myself *mostly* in check.

Though that want to follow her lead didn't stop the tether connecting us together from thrumming loudly inside my mind. The shared electricity practically begged me to claim her and make it so that there was never again a threat to our bond.

Dawsyn might have changed her mind seemingly overnight about me—and that was exactly what I'd hoped for—but I wouldn't bond with her until I knew she was certain. That this sudden longing wasn't just one of her moods and tomorrow would be a different story.

At least, that was what I told myself until her hands slipped under my shirts, fingers tracing over the muscles of my stomach while her nails bit into my skin.

The rumble in my chest echoed around us, and I flipped her over in one quick movement so that I was on top of her and staring down into her mischievous eyes. She nodded once and reached for my shirt again.

Fuck. I knew I should stop her, that there was a chance she'd regret taking things any further, but I couldn't. I wasn't *that* strong.

As she lifted my shirt, my lips touched lightly over the curve of her breasts and I worked at the button on her pants.

My dragon was close to the surface. So much so that I needed to be careful not to drop the cloak around me, but that was the least of my worries once I heard the door thud open, then loudly slam closed.

"What the fuck are..." River's deep voice trailed off as Dawsyn's head tilted back, looking upside down at her best friend.

"Nice to see you've decided to come back finally, but rather poor timing, don't you think?" she asked with a smirk, still breathing heavily.

I sat back, moving off of her and to the other side of the couch as I fixed my shirt that she nearly had off.

River glared between the two of us. "I sensed him in here and was worried he wasn't a welcome guest. I guess I've been wrong about a lot of things lately."

He turned around, and Dawsyn called his name, standing up. "I have something I need to tell you."

Without turning back, he replied, "Something?"

She glanced at me, and I nodded as she said, "Everything. I want to tell you everything."

He snorted and barely looked in Dawsyn's direction. "*Now* you want to. It's a little late for that, and I can see what choice you made."

His tone was filled with venom, and I knew my mate could fight her own battles, but he was being ridiculous.

"When you meet your mate, you'll look back on this and wish you'd been more understanding," I said, moving to stand next to Dawsyn. "I put Dawsyn in an impossible position. Even if she didn't want to accept me, the connection between us is difficult at best to ignore."

He didn't soften at my words, just turned and glanced between us. "It doesn't seem as if she's having a problem accepting you now."

"River, quit being an asshole and sit down so I can explain," Dawsyn said with a huff. "You know I'm sorry and I want to tell you everything now."

He crossed his arms like a child. "Maybe it's too late *now*."

She stalked forward and grabbed the back of his neck, pushing him away from the door. "Too late? You're going to throw away over two decades of friendship because I wasn't ready to tell you that I had a mate? Get over yourself. I'm done taking the blame for this. Yes, I could have told you, but I shouldn't have had to before I was ready. I could kick your ass for making me feel otherwise."

Dawsyn had led him to the table and forced him down onto one of two chairs next to their kitchen area.

He didn't fight her, which was good for both their sakes. I didn't want to punch my mate's best friend, but I wasn't above it if he continued to treat her like trash.

I sat back down on the couch. I wasn't going to leave in case River had questions she wasn't sure how to answer, but I didn't need to intrude on their conversation.

Dawsyn took the chair next to him, moving it until they were facing each other. "Cillian isn't a hybrid."

A crease formed between his brows, and he took a subtle inhale. "What the hell is he then?"

She glanced at me, and I nodded again. If I was going to have all of Dawsyn, then I needed to be okay with the fact that it wasn't just her I was accepting into my life.

"He's a dragon shifter," she answered, looking River right in the eyes.

Only, he didn't take her seriously. He laughed darkly and sneered. "You expect me to believe *that's* the secret you've been keeping?"

She crossed her arms and narrowed her eyes. "Yes, because I'm your best friend and you should trust me."

"Trust goes both ways, D," he said with only slightly less attitude than before.

I got up and closed the distance between us in three strides. I purposely stood closer than necessary, a rumble in my chest. "I can only do this for a few seconds so watch closely."

With precise control, I held my arm out and closed my eyes until the magic of the cloak showed itself in the form of an opaque shield within my mind.

With steadied concentration, I revealed the true scent of my dragon heritage, darker and earthier than the hybrid version I'd been imitating. Quicker than I expected, scales pushed through my skin, covering nearly my entire arm. I looked at River, and his jaw dropped.

I swiftly forced the cloak back over my body, and my brownish-green colored scales disappeared in the same second.

"What the fuck?" he muttered.

Dawsyn chuckled. "More like what the dragon, but do you understand now why it wasn't just about me not telling you that I'd found my mate? This is so much bigger than just me and Cillian."

"He's not the only one?" River's eyes widened. I went back to the couch, no longer feeling the need to intimidate him.

"No, there's an entire realm of them," I answered once I was seated.

"*Realm*?" he questioned.

Dawsyn nodded. "Like Fae Islands. Only this one is for dragon shifters and it's under attack by something they can't figure out. That's why Cillian is here. He's looking for a spell to help locate who or what is causing the mayhem in Drago."

River's hands rubbed over his face several times, then pulled at his hair. "I need a minute."

Dawsyn kicked his shin, a grin on her face. "Don't you feel like an asshole now?"

He glared at her. "Shut up."

I assumed this was how they got along based on Dawsyn's smile, but still decided to cut in one last time before I gave them some time to chat alone.

"You can't tell anyone what Dawsyn shares with you," I said. "At least until I've gone back home and fixed the problems there."

River's suspicions returned. "You're going to leave Dawsyn or..."

"We haven't gotten that far yet," she said before he could make any assumptions. "I only just decided I didn't want to...not like him this morning."

Taking that as my cue to leave, I got up from the couch, grabbed the book I'd brought with me, and stepped toward the door. "I'm going to go read some more of this in my room. Let me know when you want to reach out to your grandmother or...talk some more."

"Talk." River snorted. "Because that's what you two were doing when I walked in ready to kill you for being in here."

"Shut up, Riv," Dawsyn snapped, then waved awkwardly at me. "I'll, um, see you soon?"

Her nervousness was a first. And adorable.

"Absolutely."

Because "soon" couldn't come soon enough for me.

Chapter Twenty-Three

DAWSYN

Watching Cillian leave this time and not wishing I could kill him was a reprieve I didn't know I needed. Giving in to my attraction for him and accepting that maybe this bond wasn't as life-ending and terrible as I'd built it up to be took a lot of weight off my shoulders.

But not because it was the easier choice. In fact, it only further complicated my life, but I was no longer afraid of losing what little control I thought I'd been searching for.

Though, not all my stresses had been properly handled. I still had my best friend to contend with.

His eyes had softened toward me, but I could tell he was still hurt. A frustrating but somewhat understandable fact.

"You doing alright with all this?" I asked him, nudging his foot with my shoe under the table.

He stared more at his hands than at me. "I still wish you would have told me instead of trying to deal with this on your own, but I'm not angry anymore."

Just as I'd suspected.

"How did you figure it out?" he asked me.

I recounted the shower incident with more details and how I'd felt something then but didn't understand what since Cillian had pissed me off so thoroughly. I then told him about the forest when my wolf and I had sensed our mate and lastly about the library when everything had come together.

"He wasn't going to tell me, I don't think," I admitted. "He never outright said that, but he knew I was his mate before I knew he was mine, thanks to the shield he can create around himself."

"Did that piss you off?" Riv asked.

I shook my head. "No, because I thought I would have been better off not knowing. I thought Cillian was ruining everything I'd been fighting for. To leave the pack, to see the world, to figure out who I am on my own. But today I realized that... Well, I don't know exactly. My heart was already softening, and then I saw a different side to him when he'd come to me with that book. I couldn't force myself to want to hate him any longer."

River reached across the table and squeezed my hand. "What can I do?"

"I don't know," I replied. "He thinks he's found a solution for his realm, and before you walked in, I'd already told him I needed to tell you everything. We're also going to need GiGi's help." He winced, and I laughed. "I know. I already warned Cillian that she's a unique witch, but he doesn't seem afraid."

"He's stupider than he looks," River joked.

I shoved him lightly. "Hey, no mate of mine is stupid."

His eyes cast down again. "You mentioned Brixley before. Did you really tell her first?"

"Yes and no," I admitted. "She called me with a vision. Something about me being in trouble, but also being right where I was supposed to be. She saw scales and fire and put the pieces together. Given she was seeing something about me, I didn't want to lie and say I had no idea what she was talking about. Though, I'm not sure what to do about the last thing she saw."

River sat up straighter, and his grip around my hand tightened. "What was it? Are you still in danger?"

I shrugged. "I don't know about the second question, but the first one is complicated. Especially given my change of heart." I swallowed thickly and my stomach churned furiously even thinking about what she saw. "She said that I was going to have a chosen mate. Not a fated mate."

I still think she didn't read the situation right, my wolf finally chimed in. *His dragon spirit has been mine before. We were meant to be together again, and you chose him in the end.*

She was right, and I hoped like hell that was true, but something still wasn't sitting right with me, so I'd remain cautious of what was to come.

We'll figure things out as they come, I replied as River finally processed what I'd said.

"Shit, D," he said. "No wonder you've been a mess. I'm sorry I wasn't more understanding. I just didn't know and there was this distance between us. I let my ego get the better of me."

I got up and sat on his lap, placing my head on his shoulder and wrapping my arms around him. "It's okay.

You're still my best friend, and I promise, moving forward, that I will tell you everything I can just as soon as I can."

He leaned his forehead against mine. "I promise to be more understanding, too. I don't like fighting with you. Or sleeping on different couches."

I laughed and punched his chest. "You're such an idiot. You should have come home."

"I didn't want to fight with you, and I wasn't ready to make up with you," he said. "But I'm glad I came back today. Though, I was prepared to kick Cillian's ass, not to see," he shuddered, "whatever the hell that was."

I got up from his lap and shook my head with a wide smile on my face. "It's not like you're a virgin. Don't be such a prude."

His lips flattened. "I'm not. You're like my sister. I don't want to see that shit."

"It's not like we were going to have sex right there on the couch," I defended, even though that was probably exactly where things were headed.

"Uh huh. Whatever you need to tell yourself to feel better about falling for your mate," he teased.

I wasn't sure if I'd completely fallen for my mate just yet, but I certainly wasn't going to deny the way he made my heart race or how much my fingers begged to touch every inch of him.

Finally giving into those wants and needs? It was more than I could have imagined after finding out I had a mate.

I would have told you so if you hadn't been so stubborn, my wolf chided.

Yeah, I could agree with her there, but even though I considered us one person most of the time, I'd needed to get there with Cillian on my own. She had the past connection to his spirit to make the decision easy. I hadn't had that.

"So, what now?" River asked. "Cillian said the two of you hadn't figured out logistics, but you can't tell me you're winging this whole situation."

No, I wasn't, but I was also ignoring a decent amount of it.

"I wish I could tell you that I knew," I said, "but I really don't. I only admitted my feelings an hour ago. I wasn't taking into account that he's from a different realm and that my family doesn't know his kind exists. I just..."

"You just wanted him," River finished for me, a sappy smile on his face. "I'm happy for you, D. I really am."

Ugh. We were getting all mushy. This wasn't us. Hell, this wasn't me. I didn't do feelings like this. That was probably another reason why I'd fought the bond like I had, but I was done lying to myself.

I was choosing to be more giddy than terrified of the unknown.

"There's nothing wrong with just seeing how things go for now," River said, "but if you think you're moving to another realm, you're going to have a lot of people objecting."

I wanted to disagree with him, because it would make parts of this situation easier, but I was also very aware of how lucky I was to have such an amazing family.

They'll understand, no matter what we decide, my wolf said.

I wasn't so sure about that, and all these thoughts were taking things a little too fast for me. I didn't know what we were going to do about logistics, and just because

I was done resisting him didn't mean I was diving headfirst into a life with Cillian without considering all scenarios. We had time, and I was going to take advantage of that.

"I think we need to focus on saving his realm before we make any big decisions," I said. "Do you remember GiGi's silver chalice?"

He raised a brow. "The one she put in a glass case after you put juice in it for a tea party? Of course I do. Seeing the perfect Dawsyn get yelled at was a highlight in my childhood."

I glared at him but also laughed. "Rude."

"But true." He chuckled with me. "What about it?"

"An image of it, along with a few other things, was in the book Cillian had brought over earlier," I said. "GiGi was also mentioned in the passage about the spell Cillian wants to use."

"So, you're going to call her and what?" he asked. "Try to lie to the most powerful witch in existence? You can't be so distracted with your mate that you think that's going to work, which means you plan on telling her the truth. But you know just as well as I do what will happen once you do."

She'd want to tell my parents and the others, but that was only if I didn't tell her in the right way.

"Just let me worry about that," I said. "I'm going to call her now. Do you want to hang out and say hi?"

I was tempted to ask Cillian to come back before I reached out to my grandmother, but something told me that this first conversation was better to do without him.

"I need to get to class, but tell her I said hi," he said,

getting up from the table and heading to his room. "I just needed a notebook that I didn't have with me."

A laugh bubbled out of me. "So, you weren't coming to save me or see how I was."

He shrugged. "Maybe not, but you know I would have anyway."

That I did. Fighting or not, he was still my best friend.

River grabbed what he needed and came over to where I was standing near my room. His arms wrapped tightly around me, and he pressed his lips against the side of my head. "I'm really happy you found your mate. I won't lie and say I'm excited he's a dragon shifter, but his secrets are safe with me so long as you're safe with him."

"I don't think you'll have anything to worry about when it comes to my safety," I said as we pulled apart. "You saw what he did to Jude."

River rolled his eyes. "Yeah, that doesn't make me feel better. He was acting on emotion then." He gave me another squeeze. "I missed you these few days, but I need to go. I'll see you tonight?"

I nodded with a bright grin. "Dinner. Just me and you?"

"I'll bring food back here for us," he said, then slipped out the door.

I dropped back onto the couch and let out a heavy sigh. Holy shit. My life was finally coming back together. River wasn't angry with me. I wasn't frazzled about Cillian. It was as if I was finally on the right path to figuring out who I was, just as I'd wanted.

For the first time in the two weeks since I'd left my pack, I finally felt like I could really breathe.

I pulled my phone from my back pocket and clicked on my contacts, pressing on GiGi's name. My stomach twisted due to what I was about to not only tell her, but also ask her. Though, there was likely little reason to be worried. My grandmother had a track record of doing things that pissed people off, and this would certainly do that with my parents.

"Dawsyn," she answered with suspicion. "I thought you were off living your best life. Why are you calling me?"

"Can't I just want to hear your voice?" I chuckled.

"No," she deadpanned. "What's wrong?"

I sighed. "You didn't even let me butter you up."

"I'm not a roll you're about to eat for dinner, child," she chastised. "Now, tell me. Do we have bodies to bury or a boy to turn into a toad?"

"Sorry to disappoint, GiGi, but I think I have something even better for you," I said. "Am I good to speak freely?"

"Well, I'm alone in the attic of Spell House, so I'd say yes," she replied. "What have you gotten into over there at the academy?"

"First, I need you to promise me something," I said.

I could hear the evil smirk in her voice. "Does this promise include doing fun things?"

"Knowing you, I'd say yes."

"Well, then get on with it," she urged.

I was gambling a lot by telling her, but I had to believe this wouldn't be for nothing.

Beatrix won't mess this up for us, my wolf said. *She's going to be too intrigued.*

That was what I was hoping as well.

"You need to promise not to tell my parents," I said first. "I'm handling the situation. We just need some magical help, which is why I'm calling you."

"You're an adult, Dawsyn," she replied. "I'm also not your GiGi so that I can tell on you. My job is to get you in as much trouble as possible, then send you on your way. So, tell me. How are we doing that today?"

I loved this woman so damned much.

"Thanks, GiGi," I said. "I found my mate, but he's in a bit of trouble."

She chuckled. "Of course, he is. Pack trouble?"

"Um, not exactly, but sort of," I said. I wasn't sure if the dragons would consider themselves a pack or not, but that detail probably didn't matter much.

"Is he a vampire or warlock, then?" she asked with a bit of surprise in her tone.

"Nope."

"A hybrid?"

"Not that either," I admitted.

She let out a gasp. "A *human*?"

I had to laugh at that. "No. Though, that might have been easier."

"Well, you better start explaining before I hang up," she snapped. "I'm not getting any younger over here."

"He's a dragon shifter." The words left my lips quiet, but clear.

Silence was her only response, but I'd wait for however long I needed to for her to wrap her head around the revelation.

I heard a thud in the background, followed by a few mumbled words, then stomping feet.

"I heard you right," she finally said. "You said dragon shifter."

"Yep."

"And you're sure?"

I pictured the scales I'd seen on Cillian's arms. "Very sure. My wolf also recognizes him as a mate from a past life."

"And she didn't think to inform us before this that dragons existed?" she asked, words filled with annoyance.

I thought they'd all died, my wolf said, and I repeated it back to GiGi.

"And who else knows that he's your mate or that he's even here?" she asked, then immediately added. "Is he the only one?"

"River and Brixley know," I said. "And I think he's the only one here, but he's not the only one left. There is another realm where they live. That's where the trouble is. He's here trying to find something to save his home."

She was quiet for a beat. "We shouldn't get involved in their problems."

"But it's not just their problems anymore," I replied, saying what I'd known from the moment I realized he was my mate. Even if I hadn't wanted to admit it at the time.

"No, I guess not," she said. "What do you think I can do?"

"Anything, but there is something more specific I need," I said.

She scoffed. "Don't douse me in compliments. You know those don't work on me."

No, they didn't often. Beatrix knew her worth and didn't need the validation of others to help with that.

"What is this specific thing you need?" she asked.

I started to tell her about the book Cillian had and the passage I read, along with the chalice I saw drawn, but she cut me off mid-explanation.

"Where did he find that book?" she demanded.

"I don't know. I didn't ask."

Another moment of silence. "You need to go find him and call me back. No. I'll be there soon. You're still staying in River's dorm?"

"I am."

"Good," she said. "Don't talk about this out loud anymore and get back to your dorm with that shifter as soon as possible."

And then the line went dead.

Shit. I'd known this was a big deal, but I didn't think she'd react so strongly. Then again, GiGi usually did the thing everyone least expected.

I got up from the couch and went in search of Cillian. For the first time since meeting him, the thought of seeing him didn't bring me an ounce of dread. Though, he might not feel the same about me once I introduced him to my grandmother...

Chapter Twenty-Four

CILLIAN

I'd gone back to my room after leaving Dawsyn's and decided to scour the book once more, only much slower than the previous times. Each time I reread a passage, I felt like I was learning something new, and the possibility of saving our realm seemed that much closer.

In the beginning sections, there was more information on the items I'd seen in the image under the surge spell. Information that would likely be helpful in tracking them down if we couldn't get Dawsyn's grandmother to help.

Speaking of... Her scent hit me moments before I heard her knock. I was up and off my bed just as her knuckles hit the wood.

I opened up to find her grinning on the other side. "This is weird."

My head tilted to the side. "What is?"

"Coming to you and not wishing you'd disappear."

Her honesty was something I would never get tired of.

"Well, I won't complain about weird then," I said, then gestured for her to come in.

She shook her head. "We need to go back to my dorm. Someone is meeting us there."

"Who would that be?"

A grimace formed on her face. "I'm not supposed to say anything else, but bring that with you."

I glanced back where she pointed at the nightstand beside my bed where I'd left the book. "Okay."

She was being cryptic, but I didn't question her. Something must have come up when she was talking to River.

I grabbed the book and went back to her side. I was tempted to wrap an arm around her and kiss her, but decided better of it when I saw her shifting her gaze between my door and the direction of hers.

"Are you okay?" I asked as I closed up behind me.

She nodded. "Yep."

Her voice squeaked, so I stopped her, grabbing her wrist and pulling her closer to me. "Dawsyn. What the hell happened?"

She glanced around and lowered her voice. "I hope you really meant that I could tell my grandmother about you because I might have called her, and she might be waiting in my dorm as we speak."

That hadn't been what I expected her to say, but I wasn't mad about it.

"That's good," I said reassuringly. "Let's go meet her."

She stayed put and bit her lower lip. "I wasn't nervous until I knocked on your door. Just don't take anything she says personally. Sometimes she's not the most...compassionate."

I stroked her cheek with the back of my fingers. "I can

already tell she's important to you. I promise I won't let her piss me off and say something to put you in a bad position."

This woman was a grandmother. She couldn't *be* that bad.

Then again, if she was anything like my Nannio, maybe I should have been heeding Dawsyn's words.

Before her panic could get worse, I leaned further in and kissed her. She gasped in surprise, but then grabbed on to my shirt, anchoring herself to me.

I'd intended to make the kiss brief, but she opened her mouth to me, and I couldn't stop myself from tasting her again.

My hands cupped her face, angling it to the left as I deepened the kiss. She groaned beneath my touch and then yelped, scaring the hell out of me.

"I don't like to be kept waiting," a woman's voice called out from behind us.

Dawsyn rubbed her ass cheek. "Damn it, GiGi. Was that necessary?"

An older woman dressed in a cream linen outfit winked a green eye at us. "Yep. Now, hurry up."

She turned on a heel, her long silver hair floating behind her, but I didn't pay her much attention. "Are you okay?" I asked Dawsyn.

"Yeah. She just shocked my ass. Nothing new." She grabbed my hand. "Come on before she comes back."

She pulled me down the hallway and around the corner to the dorm she shared with River. The door was cracked open. When we entered, her grandmother was waiting behind the door.

She popped out as if she was trying to scare us. "Hold still."

The older witch rubbed her hands together, silver mist forming around them, then she pressed a palm over each of our chests.

Chills raced through me. I tried to step back, but it was as if she'd attached herself to me. Seconds later, we were released with a light shove.

"If anyone planted anything magical on you, it's gone now," she said. "Let me just block the room."

I raised a brow at Dawsyn, silently wondering if all of this was really necessary, but she just shrugged.

If she trusted this woman, I would find a way to as well. Just like I'd done with River.

I followed Dawsyn to the couch while the witch finished pushing her energy around the room.

I'd been at the academy for nearly a month, and I'd yet to sense power as strong as what I felt from Beatrix. The energy made my dragon restless, but not intolerably so.

Once she was done, she grabbed a chair from the table and moved it until she was able to sit in front of us. Her eyes stared hard at me. "Where did you get the magic to hide your true self?"

"From myself," I answered.

She glared harder. "How?"

"With my scales. They give us certain benefits."

Her fingers drummed over her loose pants. "Interesting. You're going to give me one. No, a dozen of them and a pint of your blood."

"No," I snarled without thinking.

She cocked a brow. "You're telling *me* no? Did Dawsyn not tell you who I am?"

"She did, but that doesn't mean you get to demand parts of me like I'm something to be pieced apart." I calmed my voice as best I could. "Where I'm from, help doesn't have to be a two-way street."

She laughed hauntingly. "Well, we're not in your home, are we? I don't know you, Cillian. I have no way to trust you. If you want my help—which you very much need, by the way—then you better give me something in return. I don't help strangers for no reason."

"He's not really a stranger," Dawsyn said. "He's my mate. As you already know."

It was the first time I'd heard her refer to me as her mate in a protective way, and damn if it didn't make me want to kiss her senseless.

"That doesn't make him family," the old witch replied. "Not yet, anyway."

"I'll give you five scales and one vial of blood," I said, not wanting to waste time in an argument I was never going to win. "If my realm is saved, I will give you more. Within reason."

Her bright stare sparked with intrigue. "I can deal with reason. Now, hand me that stolen book and tell me who gave it to you so I can turn them to dust."

That had my eyes widening. "*This* was stolen?"

She reached forward and snatched it from me. "Yes. About thirty years ago from my coven. I never did find out who took it, but there's no expiration date for retribution."

I was beginning to realize that Dawsyn hadn't exaggerated *at all* about her grandmother.

"A student here gave it to me, but he took it from Professor Hayes," I answered, uncaring what she did to the man after he'd lied to me.

"A professor had my book?" she said darkly. "Interesting. Don't repeat that to anyone, and if the person that gave this to you asks about it, tell him it was worthless."

I hesitated to say something that would piss her off, but decided it was better she knew now. "He was a hybrid that can tell if someone is lying. I don't think I can tell him that, but I also don't think he'll ask questions."

"Hmmm." She turned the book over in her lap. "Maybe I'll need this student's help, but first, tell me what you think you can use inside of here."

I pointed to all the tabs. "The one with the asterisk marked at the end. It talks about something called *The Surge*. I want to use that in my realm to stop who or whatever is attacking it."

Beatrix's lips thinned as she flipped to the page in question. Her eyes moved over the words and images, and her expression only continued to get grimmer.

"I've read this one before, but I haven't seen it enacted," she said. "I can find what you'll need, but you're going to need a different witch. I won't be going to the dragon realm."

Saying what I was about to was a risk, but I was beginning to see nothing was going to get done if I didn't trust the people I needed help from.

"I won't need a witch," I said. "Just the items shown and then my scales can take care of the rest."

Her brows nearly went to her hairline. "What the hell does that mean?"

"It means that under certain circumstances, dragon scales have magical properties," I answered. "It's why we've been hidden for so long. People didn't like that we were capable of so much and wanted our scales for their own greed."

She chuckled. "And of course, I proved that nothing here has changed by doing the same."

At least she wasn't oblivious.

"Just so you know, I'd never take them from you," Beatrix said. "I'd bargain for them to the point of blackmail, but I'd never forcefully take them."

I wasn't sure that was much different, but she seemed to think so and decided to leave it at that.

She glanced at Dawsyn. "Are you going to go with him when he does this spell?"

"I don't know," my mate answered, then looked at me. "We haven't discussed it."

"She can't enter Drago without being officially bonded to me," I said. "We're not in a rush, so it's likely she'll be staying here."

"Then, you'll be back to…" Beatrix's words trailed.

It seemed as if everyone close to Dawsyn wanted to know if I intended to run off with their wolf shifter.

"Like she said, we haven't discussed it," I answered. "My dying realm and the newness of the bond has held priority."

"Right," Beatrix drawled. "Well, I won't tell Roman and Cait what I know for now, but if this mess comes here, I won't be able to keep this secret for long. Your shield is rather powerful, so you're at least not upsetting the balance, but if that changes, so does our agreement."

"I understand," I said. "And I appreciate your help and discretion."

"Now, about the payment." She pulled a vial from her left front pocket. "Do you want to poke or can I?"

Something told me the crazy witch would get too much enjoyment out of stabbing me. I opted to take care of it myself.

"Is the room guarded enough that I can lower my cloak here?" I asked. This wasn't going to be the same as just quickly showing River earlier. If I was pulling scales, I needed to do a partial shift that would emit more dragon energy than I was comfortable with in the dorms. "Normally, I only do so in the forest furthest from the school."

She scoffed. "You're perfectly safe right here."

I didn't exactly agree with her, considering how her eyes watched my every move, but that didn't stop me from dropping the shield and allowing my dragon energy to unfurl around me.

Beatrix's stare widened, and Dawsyn sucked in a breath. I tried to ignore both so I could get this payment over with.

I took the vial and a knife from the witch, stabbing my palm, then tilting the glass opening under the wound. I moved my hand until the blood began dripping down, dark crimson in color.

My gaze flicked over to Dawsyn. Her pulse was going crazy, and she was staring at me hard while biting her inner cheek.

A blush coated her cheeks, and her chest expanded. I could scent her growing attraction and couldn't deny my own was increasing by the second. I nearly let the vial drop from my fingers and completely forgot we weren't alone as my body instinctually leaned closer to her. At least, until Beatrix spoke up.

"You keep that up and I'm tempted to either drop the shield around this room or throw up on you." She gagged. "Hell, I might do both just for the fun of it."

The vial was full enough, so I shoved it back at her. "If you vomit on me, there won't be any scales for you."

She cackled. "Right, because you're in the position of power here."

Fuck. She wasn't wrong.

I did my best to block out Dawsyn, then encouraged my dragon to come forward. Earthy brown scales with a few splashes of teal appeared on my arms, and my fingernails extended into the claws that I'd need to pluck the scales out.

"Fascinating," Beatrix said softly.

This might be "fascinating" to them, but it was going to hurt like hell for me.

I dug a claw into the first scale and jerked it to the right, wincing as it ripped from my skin, a small amount of blood pooling where the scale had just been. This was much easier when I was fully shifted, but I didn't have that luxury at the moment.

Without dragging it out, I yanked three more from my forearm until I had sweat pooling around my neck.

"Are you okay?" Dawsyn asked, her hand landing on my thigh and providing the perfect distraction I needed to get the fifth one without having to make a noise.

I dropped the last one into Beatrix's waiting hand and forced my scales to disappear before rubbing my palm over my arm where there were five wounds, healing quickly enough that I only needed a towel to wipe up the few drops of blood. "I'm fine."

"You're in pain, but I applaud your strength," the witch said. "Maybe you'll be a better match for my granddaughter than I originally suspected."

Her comment annoyed me, but I held my tongue and got up to clean up my arm.

By the time I turned back around, Beatrix was also standing and staring hard at the book I'd given her. When I rejoined Dawsyn on the couch, the old witch nodded at her. "I'll be in touch. Don't go anywhere you don't belong and stay away from the professor. I haven't decided how I want to handle him."

"Easy enough," my mate said. "I'm not taking any classes here."

Beatrix pointed between us. "The two of you should stay away from as many people as you can. You should even consider leaving the school. I also shouldn't be keeping this secret, but I'll honor your wishes until this realm business is resolved or worsened."

Dawsyn stood and hugged her. "Thank you, GiGi. I knew I could count on you."

The witch didn't return her hug. "Yeah, yeah. I need to go before anyone realizes I left and tries to figure out where I went. Again, don't do anything stupid before you hear back from me. Even better, just stay right here in this room. The shield won't keep anyone out, but it will hold until the door is opened."

She turned around and moved her hands in a circular motion until a portal began to open. On the other side was a dark room filled with shelves of books and a black cauldron. She stepped through and waved once before the swirling edges of the opening started to shrink in on itself until the opening no longer existed.

That was magic I'd never seen before in Drago, but I'd at least read about it growing up. The books hadn't done it justice, and I suddenly wondered if dragons could learn to replicate the magic somehow. Though, our inner beasts wouldn't be too happy if we began plucking scales on a daily basis.

Before I turned to look at Dawsyn again, I started to put my shield back up, not only out of habit, but because even though Beatrix felt confident that I was safe in this room, I didn't want to chance River walking in again and breaking the spell. Not when I was so close to getting the answers I needed.

Except as I started to call on the cloaking energy, Dawsyn placed her hand on my chest. "Wait."

She stepped closer to me, and I was almost certain I'd stopped breathing.

Chapter Twenty-Five

DAWSYN

I'd only had a glimpse of our bond a couple of times, but standing next to Cillian with his guard down more than I'd ever seen it, I was in awe. Hell, I was falling into an abyss and had no desire to be saved.

My skin itched, my wolf howled inside my head, my heart raced, and my body yearned to touch every part of him.

I placed a hand over his chest and closed my eyes, soaking up the connection. If I'd felt this before...this strongly...it might have changed everything, but then again, the last couple weeks hadn't been so bad.

My wolf lightly scoffed.

Okay, they were kind of terrible, but I was certain that those shitty days were only making me appreciate the pulsing of our bond I felt wrapping around me even more.

The ebb and flow between us was strong, taking my breath away and giving it back all at once. I needed Cillian then more than I'd ever needed anything in my life.

The desire to be there for him, to support him in any

way that I could, was all-consuming.

When I reopened my eyes, he was staring down at me, a glow within his gaze that had me holding tighter to him.

"Have you felt the connection this strongly the whole time?" I asked reverently.

He shook his head. "No, but as soon as you touched me with my cloak down…"

There weren't any words needed. I'd understood exactly what he meant.

"We might not know what comes next, but I won't be walking away from you. No matter what happens," he said, raising his hands to hold my face gently between his palms. As if I was made from glass and the most precious thing he'd ever touched.

I leaned into his warmth, soaking in the connection, the need, the unfiltered want. "I'm sorry I was such a bitch before."

He shook his head, then gave me a half-smirk. "Don't talk about my mate like that. There's no reason for apologies."

I didn't agree. I'd been selfish and unwilling to see any other options than what I'd originally planned in my head. So much of my life had been mapped out for me, and I'd hated it so much that I'd left my pack. Then, I went and did the same thing. To myself. I set one path and thought deviating from it was wrong, but I could see differently now. There was no way that I'd have ever figured out who I was on my own by trying to control every aspect of my life just so that someone else couldn't.

I could still find myself and not be alone.

There was nothing wrong with that, and I wasn't going

to fight against the pull I felt toward my mate. Not again.

I pushed up onto my toes and wrapped my arms around Cillian's neck. My stare bored into his, matching the desire I could see pulsing within his dark-grey eyes.

His lips pressed against mine. Once, twice, then a third time when I held him tightly in place. My tongue moved along the crease of his mouth, then pushed forward, tasting the sweetness of him.

He slowly trailed his hands from my face and down my sides, then to my ass. He bent forward, getting a better grip on me before lifting me up.

My legs wrapped around his waist, and he pushed me against the wall.

Warmth filled my core, and I locked my ankles around his back, needing to be as close to him as possible.

He deepened the kiss only to move away from my mouth and down my neck, scraping his teeth over my neck and sending shivers down my spine, all the way to my toes.

Need unfurled within me, and I started yanking at his shirt, ripping it once my frustration became too strong. I slid my hands over his muscled skin. The dark outline of scales appeared everywhere my palms touched, creating a path over his shoulders and down his arms, but they never broke the skin.

Cillian's mouth captured mine again, a rumble in his chest echoing around us as his hands squeezed my ass.

I kissed him hard, soaking in the connection to him, knowing that as soon as we stopped, he was going to hide himself from the rest of our world again. I wasn't ready to lose this.

Not yet. Maybe not ever.

My nails grazed over his chest, and vibrations moved between us, but I couldn't tell if they were from his dragon or my wolf.

"Dawsyn," Cillian whispered my name over my lips, but it sounded more like a warning.

I shook my head, kissing him again. We still had time. The shield from Beatrix would hold.

"If you keep kissing me like this, I'm going to have to take you back to Drago so that I can really have my way with you," he said, ending the kiss, but making me grin.

"You say that as if it's a threat you expect me to be concerned with," I replied, my lips pressing against his neck, then his shoulder.

"You should be," he said. "I can't take you to Drago without initiating the bond."

I glanced back up at him and raised a brow. "And how would we do that?"

For wolf shifters, we bonded with sex and sometimes by biting each other. The exact process depended on if both mates were wolves and if they were fated or chosen mates.

He lifted one hand, skimming the back of his knuckles over my cheek, then across my collarbone. "Well, it involves a knife, some blood, and scales. How does that sound?"

I let out a light laugh. "Messy and painful." I was also surprised it didn't involve sex like it did for all the other supernaturals I knew.

"It shouldn't be either when it's done right," he whispered, kissing me softly. "But we're not rushing anything. You've only just changed your mind. Not that I want to give you time to rethink things again, but I won't have a mate with regrets."

A part of me wanted to swoon at how thoughtful he was being, but a much larger part of me wanted to strangle him.

He's our mate, my wolf said reverently. *He'll always do what's best for us, even if we don't like it.*

I wasn't sure I believed her. Nobody was perfect. Mate or not, mistakes happened, but we were both riding a high from allowing the bond to seep into us so thoroughly. I chose not to disagree for once. With either of them.

"What now?" I asked, still keeping my ankles locked around his back, enjoying the delicious throb of him between my legs.

He pushed my hair behind my ear and stroked his thumb across my cheek. "Now, I need to leave."

My body tensed against him. "Excuse me?"

"With what we learned today and the fact that I can't get a hold of my grandmother or my uncle, I need to return to Drago," he said. "But it will be quick. No more than three days."

An unhappy grumble built in my chest. "I don't like it, but I'll try to understand."

He kissed me again. "Just stay close to River and try not to leave the room if you're going to be alone."

"Why?" I asked. "Do you agree with Beatrix and think there's going to be trouble here?"

"She seemed more than conflicted about the professor," he answered. "I think we're digging into things that the world would rather leave buried, and we can't be too careful."

Unfortunately, he probably wasn't wrong.

"It's a good thing I've yet to look for a job or consider

any of the classes," I teased, trying to lighten the mood.

I didn't like the idea of having just decided to give our bond a real shot and then parting with him on a dark note.

He loosened his hold on me. "It's a very good thing."

I slid down the front of his body. "So, you're leaving..."

"Now." He frowned. "I want to be back before Beatrix finds anything. I could wait for her, but I need to warn my family of what's coming. They'll need to prepare people to fight if needed."

I knew he was right, but that didn't mean I liked it. Though, I tried to keep those feelings to myself.

Until he put his cloak back up.

My hand pressed over his chest. There was still a slight twinge there, but it was nothing like moments before when the tether between us had felt so tangible. Like I could have grabbed it with my hands and never let go. It practically cut me to the bone with disappointment. "This is... It sucks."

His forehead moved to rest against mine. "It does, but hopefully I only have to hide for a short time."

Hell. I hoped so.

We kissed again—not nearly long enough—and then he was heading to the door.

I stayed where I was, watching his every step and already missing the thrum of our bond.

As soon as he opened the door, I sensed the shield around the dorm fall. Our little bubble of whatever that was had officially—and literally—popped.

He glanced back one last time, his eyes roaming over every inch of my body as if I was standing naked before him and he was memorizing every part of me. "I'll be back as soon as I can be."

"You better be," I said, then smirked. "Or I might just have to find me another shifter."

A darkness I'd yet to see from him passed over his eyes, and the metal of the doorknob groaned from his tightened grip.

"I'd fucking kill them," he seethed, chest rising and falling rapidly.

"Kidding, Cillian," I said, closing the distance between us again for one last kiss. "Just hurry."

He nodded stiffly, then disappeared before either of us could do something we probably shouldn't.

I walked toward the couch and dropped down onto it. My head hit the cushion, and I threw an arm over my eyes, grumbling, "What the hell am I supposed to do now?"

I'd not only admitted my feelings for Cillian, but I'd grabbed on to our bond and allowed its power to suck me in with no regrets.

I had a mate, and for the first time, I wasn't at all mad about that fact.

Which makes your wolf happy, too, she said. *But we're not going to be able to stay in this room for three days. I'm going to need to run after all this.*

I could feel her pent-up energy pulsing inside me and knew she was right. If I didn't get to the forest, she was going to be in pain.

As soon as River is back for dinner, we'll go for a run, I promised.

My phone began ringing, the noise seeming louder than normal and causing me to jump. I reached for it and saw Brixley's name on the screen.

"Shit."

I didn't want to answer, especially after what had just transpired with Cillian, but I knew it was better to know what Brix had seen than to remain oblivious.

"Hey," I said, bringing the phone to my ear.

"Are you okay?" she asked quickly.

"Yep. What did you sense?"

Please don't be something to do with Cillian, I thought.

There was a short pause before she answered me. "Nothing. Well, not in the normal sense. I don't know. I just felt like I needed to call you. Did something happen?"

She already knew more than she was supposed to, but I didn't think telling her anything else before we'd worked out the realm mess was a good idea. Especially while Beatrix was digging into things.

"Nope," I lied. "Everything has been pretty boring here."

"And the...your new friend?" she asked. "Is he still around?"

"He is."

Neither of us said anything more, and I wasn't going to budge on my decision to keep quiet.

"Alright," she finally broke the silence. "If you're okay, then I guess I'll let you go."

"What about you?" I asked. "You didn't sound good last we talked. Has anything gotten better with whatever that was?"

She sighed into the phone. "Yeah, it's fine. Some people are just weird when I have my...moments. When I'd felt those things about you before, I'd been in public."

"And someone said something to you?" What the hell was wrong with people? There was no such thing as normal anymore. The fact some supernaturals still shied away from the hybrids or anyone who seemed a little...different annoyed the fuck out of me.

"Not to me," she answered. "It's fine, though. I don't care."

"Well, I do," I snapped. I'd be talking with Beatrix about this shit. Someone needed to stand up for Brixley if she wasn't going to do it herself, because she was too damn nice for her own good.

"Thank you for caring, but seriously, everything is fine," she said with a bit more confidence.

"If you say so," I replied. Though, that didn't change my plans. "You better call me if that changes. I'll make you open a portal and show me anyone who has tried to make you feel less about yourself. My wolf will have no problem with biting a few heads off."

She chuckled, and it almost sounded as if she'd sniffled. "Thanks, D. I miss when we were little and got to hang out more."

Yeah, so did I.

"As soon as River gets a break from classes, we'll plan something," I promised.

That seemed to cheer her up. "I'd love that."

We said our goodbyes, and I let out a yawn. Damn it. It wasn't even lunch time, but I was exhausted from all the varying emotions.

A nap sounded like a grand idea and a perfect way to take my mind off the thought of Cillian leaving me for three days. I had to hope that I didn't feel like shit again from his absence.

Chapter Twenty-Six

CILLIAN

Going back to my dorm after being with Dawsyn and no walls between us was painful at best. My dragon swirled inside me, growing unhappier with every step I took away from our mate.

I understood his discomfort, but if we wanted to truly be with her, then the mess in Drago needed to be sorted first.

I wasn't going to abandon everything because I'd found her. That wasn't the kind of man I wanted to be for her. I would if that was my only choice, but there was a part of me that couldn't wait to get Dawsyn back to Drago. I could only do that if I found a solution.

The thought of showing her my home, to allow my dragon the time he deserved with her, to show her what I was fully capable of was all the motivation I needed to continue on the path I'd already started.

Once again, I tried mind-linking with Nannio and then Uncle Jerome. When neither of them responded, I punched my dresser, frustrated that there was no other way to get in touch with the others in our clan, thanks to the mind-linking only working between blood family members.

A knot formed in my stomach as I thought of how quickly things could have worsened back home.

As much as I didn't want to be that far from my mate, she was at least safe here. The others in Drago weren't. I had to stick with my decision to go home.

I started to pack a bag, only grabbing three days' worth of clothes and other miscellaneous items I'd need, including food for the drive.

A part of me considered asking Dawsyn to have her grandmother come back and teleport me, but Beatrix was hopefully already looking into the spell for us. I didn't want to pull her away from that or give others a reason to ask questions about her absence like she'd mentioned before.

Too bad I hadn't made friends with any witches while I'd been here.

With my bag packed, I gave one last look around my single room. It didn't have bedrooms like River and Dawsyn's. It was just one open space that fit my bed, a small couch, a table, and a half-kitchen area.

Hopefully soon, I'd never have to come back here.

I left in a hurry. The quicker I got on the road, the quicker I would be back to my mate.

My dragon at least calmed at that thought.

Uncaring of the stares I received, I ran toward the parking garage with my backpack and got to my truck. Putting in the keys, my chest twisted with agony, but there was nothing I could do to avoid leaving Dawsyn. Not yet anyway.

I started the engine, pulled out of the parking spot, and headed for the main gate. The stabbing sensation in my heart returned, but I ignored the ache as best I could, racing toward the highway that would lead to the interstate out of Washington.

Eight hours was a long fucking drive to Montana.

Once on the interstate, I sucked in an irritable breath, pressing my foot down harder on the gas pedal.

Just thirty minutes from the school, my hands were already shaking and my chest seemed as if it was caving in on my lungs. Forcing air to move through my body the way it was supposed to was painful at best, but I kept at it. If I didn't keep my focus, this trip would only take longer.

Just as I began to see more clearly, a blast of unknown energy pulsed around me, causing me to slam on the brakes and pull over.

"What the fuck was that?" I muttered inside the otherwise empty cab of my truck.

I glanced around. There were a few cars on the road, but nobody else was pulling over, as if I'd been the only one to feel whatever the hell that was.

My dragon began to thrash around inside me, the force feeling as though he was physically punching me from inside my own body.

"What the hell is wrong with you?" I asked, and then it hit me.

The only thing that could possibly make my dragon panic like that was Dawsyn.

Damn it. I hated not being able to talk to him, but the moment I thought about turning around and going back to the academy, he calmed. I took that as confirmation I was understanding his erratic behavior.

Without thinking twice, I put the truck back in drive and cut across the four-lane highway, uncaring about the people who honked or flipped me off.

I needed to get back to my mate.

I pushed the truck hard. Within twenty minutes, we were ripping back into the school and headed right for the dorm.

Not once had I sensed that same energy again, and there was nothing out of the ordinary besides my erratic thoughts that I could see around the dorms, but something still twisted inside me.

Without turning off the ignition, I leapt from the truck and raced into Baker House. My legs had me up the stairs and to the second floor in the blink of an eye.

Her door was locked, but one forceful twist and it popped open. "Dawsyn!" I called out just before I saw her body lying on the couch.

My heart sank, and I nearly dropped to my knees. She couldn't be... What would have been the loudest roar in existence began to build inside, then I saw the soft rise and fall of her chest.

I stepped closer and let out a staggered breath. She was only sleeping.

What the fuck was wrong with me? I would have heard her heart beating if I hadn't lost my shit so thoroughly.

My dragon was still very much at attention, but I could sense his confusion. It didn't seem as if either of us knew what had driven us back here. To see our mate safe and sleeping—like the dead, no less—eased the panic, but didn't take away the fear.

Was this how I was going to live the rest of my life? I hoped not, but even if it was, as long as I found Dawsyn okay just like this each time I lost my shit, it would all be worth it.

I walked closer to her, kneeled next to the couch, and pressed my lips lightly to her forehead. She had to be exhausted to have slept through all of that, which meant waking her up only to leave her again wasn't an option.

My eyes looked over her body once more, then I turned back for the door I'd broken. Shit. *That* was a problem.

I pulled it closed and it stayed that way, at least. Since I had no tools to fix the handle and no time to stay, I went back inside her room and wrote her a note on the whiteboard they had on the wall, Only writing that her lock was busted and leaving my phone number for her to call me when she was awake.

I could explain later when I had come up with a reason that didn't make me sound completely insane for racing back to the academy.

Leaving was ten times harder than it had been the first time. By the time I got back to my still-running truck, I was sweating and my dragon was back to raging inside me.

Fuck, maybe I shouldn't go.

Yet, as soon as I had that thought, I pictured my family. The image my brain conjured of our world burning around them was all the motivation I needed to get back in the truck.

That motivation ebbed and flowed with every thought

that raced through my head as I turned around and headed back toward the highway.

Something was wrong, and there was no way for me to know what I was about to find, but there was a part of me that couldn't let go of the need to get back to Drago.

Chapter Twenty-Seven

DAWSYN

That had been the best sleep I'd had since I left home. I wasn't sure if it was because I'd finally stopped fighting fate or because exhaustion had merely caught up with me, but either way, the nap had been needed.

My eyes slowly blinked open, but then something started to taste bad inside my mouth. Without moving too much, I glanced around the room, but nobody was there that I could see.

Do you sense anything? I asked my wolf.

Not inside, but you're right that something is off, she answered, not making me feel any better.

I sat up and searched the room, noticing that the door wasn't positioned as it should have been and there was a new note on the white board. One from Cillian.

He'd come back? How had I not woken up? *Shit.* I must have been more tired than I realized.

His note merely confirmed my door was broken and to call him. I shook my head and grinned. He wasn't the first overprotective male I'd been around. I'd seen that kind of behavior from my dad and the mates of my aunts on several occasions.

I couldn't deny, the image of him bursting into my room warmed my chest, and I wished I would have woken up to see it with my own eyes.

Either way, I grabbed my phone, then cringed. It was four in the afternoon. I'd slept for over five hours.

There was a text from Beatrix confirming she was on the right track with the spell and reminding me not to go anywhere alone. That suddenly annoyed me, because I could already feel myself getting hangry.

I continued to check over my phone for anything urgent, then dialed Cillian's number as I searched the cabinet for something to snack on until River came back to the dorm with the dinner we'd agreed on earlier.

"Dawsyn?" Cillian answered, voice tight and deep.

"Hey, are you okay?" I asked, rubbing at my chest as an ache started to grow there.

He grumbled something I didn't understand, then said. "As okay as I can be. I'm about two hours from the entry to Drago."

Abandoning the idea of food, I went back to the couch to sit down as the realization he was so far away began to settle in. "And you'll be headed back here tomorrow?"

"If at all possible, yes," he replied. "Are you okay?"

I considered his question for a few seconds too long, it seemed, because he quickly added, "I can turn around again."

Forcing myself to laugh, I replied, "No. I'm fine. Just bond adjustments. I'm sure they'll settle out soon enough."

"Not likely. I've been gone for hours and still feel like

shit," he said. "I've turned around a dozen times only to change my mind again just seconds later."

"Have you gotten a hold of your family yet?" I asked, knowing that had been weighing heavily on him before.

"No," he answered gruffly.

"I'm sure everything is fine," I said and hoped like hell it was true.

If something had happened to his family while he'd been here with me, I expected an entirely different Cillian to return back to me. If he even returned at all.

"I'm going to go before I turn around again," he murmured. "It's only prolonging my trip."

"Okay," I said, then hesitated. "Be safe."

"You, too."

The line went dead, and I stared at the screen for a few moments. Having a mate was weird. Worrying about someone in this capacity wasn't at all the same as when I'd been concerned when my father went to visit another pack that we weren't overly friendly with.

No, this was something else altogether.

Would I have felt like death if something had happened to my dad? Of course, but the thought of something happening to Cillian felt all-consuming. As if the mere fact of him just not being okay might tear me in two.

Damn it. I needed to get my head right.

Yes, I was open to the bond—craved it, even—and wasn't at all ashamed by that fact, but losing myself entirely? That wasn't going to happen.

I clicked on River's name next, but his phone went straight to voicemail. I groaned loudly. He shouldn't have still been in class this late, and I needed sustenance.

My stomach grumbled again. Maybe I could call Justine. The vampire didn't know everything that was going on, but surely, she could hold her own if shit hit the fan by me leaving my dorm to meet her in the dining hall. A little something to hold me over until River called back.

I searched for her name in my phone but paused before calling her.

I heard footsteps coming and went toward the door, hoping it was River, but before I could reach for the handle, my wolf perked up.

That's not River, she hissed. *Go out the window.*

There was no sense in questioning her. I tucked my phone in my back pocket and raced for the other side of the room. My fingers fumbled with the lock on the window as someone kicked in my already-broken door.

Who the fuck is coming after us? I asked, not really expecting an answer.

Just run!

I chanced a glance back as I shoved the window open, and there was just one man with greenish-yellow eyes, wide shoulders, long ebony hair, and a scar over his right cheek. His sneer was directed right at me, and he had the same odd hybrid energy that Cillian did with his cloak up.

I had one foot out the window when the unwelcome guest clicked his tongue loudly at me. "I wouldn't do that if I were you. Your friend's life depends on it."

That was one of the only things that could have given me pause.

I stayed straddled on the windowsill. "Which friend?" Not that I would have left Justine to die, but I still needed to know.

The creepy, assumingly dragon shifter pulled a phone from his front pocket and clicked a few buttons before turning the screen toward me.

River.

His chin was touching his chest, head lolled to the side, bruises already on his face, and his grey shirt was covered in blood splatter.

A snarl ripped from deep inside me. "I'll fucking kill you for that."

He smirked. "No, you won't. Not unless you want to kill him, too," the stranger taunted. "Now, come back inside so we can chat."

My nails dug into the wood beneath my hands. *I could track River.*

This guy is too confident, my wolf replied. *I doubt he left River alone. If we run, River could die before we find him.*

Fuck! I screamed in my head.

So much for not leaving my damn room so that trouble didn't find me.

Regrettably, I slipped back into the room, but I left the window open for a quick escape and stayed leaning against the wall.

"That's a good little bitch," he taunted.

The growl coming from my chest was all wolf. "I'd watch your words if you want your head to stay attached."

He pressed another button on the screen and showed me a new image. One with a man in all black, a ski mask over his face and a knife in his hand, which was positioned at River's throat.

"And I'd watch how you speak back to me."

Damn it. This was not going well.

"What do you want?" I asked, keeping my jaw clenched and fists tight.

He chuckled and took a seat at the table, kicking his black boots up onto the other chair. "That's a complicated question, Dawsyn, but to give you an answer, I want you."

"Excuse me?" I gaped. No fucking way was he getting *me*.

"You heard me," he said smoothly. "I know you're aware of what I am, but what you don't know is *who* I am."

"And what does that have to do with you coming here, hurting River, and acting as if you can stake claim to me like I'm a piece of property?" I asked, causing him to laugh in return.

"Oh, Dawsyn," he sighed. "I knew you were stubborn, but I didn't think you were stupid."

My nails turned to claws, cutting into my palms as I ground my teeth together. "I'm not stupid."

His gaze turned dark in a split second, and he slammed his boots back to the ground as he leaned forward, rage pulsing from him. "Then, quit saying *stupid* shit."

Great. He was psychotic. Just what I wanted to deal with.

I kept my mouth shut as he settled back into his seat. "I don't have time to placate you, so listen closely, because I'm only going to explain this once. You're going to Drago with me as my mate. You're going to help me end that pathetic excuse of a realm, and then we're going to come here and show the other supernaturals who the real alpha of your world is."

I still had no idea who this man was or why he sought me out, and with the image of River bloodied and bruised still fresh in my mind, I tried to speak as calmly as possible. "I already have a mate."

His smirk returned. "But you're not bonded to him, are you, little wolf?"

Fuck. I wasn't. With our bond incomplete, there was nothing stopping me from forming another one with someone else.

He pulled a knife from the side of his boot and stood up from the table, stalking toward me. "You're going to be my mate and do all the things I asked, or your friend is going to die. The choice is yours. You can be mine, or you can be a murderer. Just know there is no third option."

Choice... The choice was mine.

Right then, I knew exactly what I was going to do, no matter how much I hated the mere thought of doing so.

Brixley had already told me.

I was never going to reject Cillian because I wanted someone else. I was going to have a chosen mate because I had no other fucking *choice.*

River would die because of me if I didn't, and I would never survive that kind of guilt.

But I could live with the hope that if I saved my best friend, that I could also find a way to save myself.

Chosen mates weren't bonded like fated ones. This bastard couldn't hold the world over me forever. I'd find a way out or I'd die trying, but at least River wouldn't go down with me.

"Who are you?" I asked, my voice deflated now that I knew my fate.

He closed the distance between us and skimmed the blunt side of the blade over my neck. "I'm Knox. The brother Cillian never knew he had, but that he'll be meeting soon enough. Right after I take his mate from him."

What in the shittery shit was happening?

How could Cillian not know he had a brother when his parents had been gone for nearly twenty years? Obviously, I wasn't going to get an answer to that anytime soon, but damn it!

We have to go with him, my wolf said.

I know that, I replied, *but I'm surprised you agree. If we go with him, we'll be bonded to him.*

We'll figure that out later, but if we go with him, then we'll be closer to Cillian sooner, she reasoned. Though, it didn't sound like the best excuse for going through whatever hell I was about to endure.

Knox traced the blade down my arm. "What's your choice, little wolf? Be my mate or become a murderer? The clock on your friend's life is counting down."

I looked into his beady, swamp-colored eyes and nodded curtly. "I'll be your mate as long as River lives."

The grin on his face made me want to vomit nearly as much as his words did. "Good girl."

Before I could ask what was next, he snatched my wrist and flattened out my fingers so he could see my palm. "Seems you've already started the process. Glad to know you're eager to be mine."

Bile rose in my throat, and I forced myself to choke it down. I had to do this for River. I could do this to get to Cillian sooner like my wolf said. This was not my forever. I wouldn't accept that. But I would find a way to accept that Knox was my right now.

He sliced his own palm, then dropped the cloak that

kept his dragon identity concealed. Charcoal scales appeared on his forearm, and he tore one from his skin, a trickle of blood dripping from the now-empty space.

"I need the cut on your palm wide enough to fit the scale." He twirled the knife between his fingers. "I can do the honors, or you can finish the job."

"I've got it," I deadpanned, having decided it was best to just keep all emotion out of my tone when I spoke to this psycho.

My pointer finger took on my wolf's claw again and I scraped it over the previous wound I'd made on my palm, making the incision another inch bigger. "It will heal quickly," I told him, not knowing if dragons had the same perks wolves did.

"I don't need much time." His jovial voice made my stomach churn harder and my body tense.

Gods, I hoped I didn't regret this.

Oh, who was I kidding? I already did and I hadn't even bonded to the dickface yet.

He pressed the scale into the cut on my palm. Smoke began to rise around the dark shape, and I tried to tear my hand away from him, but his hold tightened.

"Not until you're mine," Knox murmured, then combined our hands.

My wolf howled inside me, and tears formed in my eyes. I tried to hold them back, but I was breaking in ways I didn't know I could.

The tether I could feel toward Cillian started turning to ash inside me. My heart was slowly and torturously shattering, and my wolf's cries weren't helping either.

I forced my eyes closed and tried to breathe through the

pain, but there was nothing in the world that could ease the ache of being stripped of the connection to my fated mate.

My muscles seized, and I couldn't move. I merely stood there, unable to be numb to the ravenous storm whipping through me.

Forgive me, I murmured to Cillian even though I knew he wouldn't hear me.

The last wisps of the bond I had with him flitted away like sand in the desert. No longer could I hold in my anguish. A roar tore from my chest, and I fell to the ground. The only thing holding me partially up was the hold Knox still had on my hand.

His energy began to enter the cavernous void inside me, but it would never fill the crater that was left behind from my connection to Cillian.

Tears tracked down my face with abandon, and my body burned with fury and grief as I tried to remember this was my only choice.

I had to save River. I had to get to Cillian.

Knox picked me up from the floor, smashed his lips against my unforgiving mouth, and laughed. "You'll come around and see that I'm the better brother," he said, then his voice darkened. "Everyone will or it will be their end."

He could believe whatever he wanted, but this was not *my* end.

This was only the beginning. I'd make damn sure of that.

Thank you so much for reading A Dragon's Wolf! I know

cliffhangers are never the greatest, but I promise, the second book A Dragon's Curse isn't too far behind! Preorder your copy HERE(link coming before release) and then join my reader group Heather Renee's Book Warriors to get early sneak peeks of what's to come!

In the meantime, make sure you've read the other Mystics and Mayhem books so you can fully enjoy all of the character cameos as the series continues! Find more about those on the next few pages.

Stay in Touch

Find Heather on Facebook:
Reader Group
Want to talk all things books and get updates before anyone else? Come hang with me in my reader group:
Heather Renee's Book Warriors

Author Page
Teaser and big updates are also posted here:
Heather Renee Author

Newsletter:
I send this out sporadically, so don't worry. You won't ever be spammed by me and you get a couple goodies when you sign up!
http://smarturl.it/HeatherReneeNL

Mystics and Mayhem

If this is your first trip into the Mystics and Mayhem, welcome! Hello again, if not :) For our first timers, the book you've just read is technically the start of the second phase within Mystics and Mayhem and the fifth series within this world!

Want to catch up with the rest of the books while you wait (hopefully) patiently for the next book? Check out the list of all the Paranormal Romance stories included in this world below. Ones where you'll always find fierce, yet relatable leading ladies and strong alpha males who sweep them off their feet, along with humor and intrigue that will keep you turning the pages.

While you don't have to read the series in any particular order as there are no spoilers between each trilogy, this is the recommended reading order:

Broken Court (Lucinda and Finn)
Dark Fae Cursed — Dark Fae Freed — Dark Fae Unrivaled
Luna Marked (Cait and Roman)

Wolf Kissed — Wolf Taken — Wolf Mated
Scorned by Blood (Amersyn and Maciah)
Vampire Heir — Vampire Ash — Vampire Vow
Fated to the Wolf (Andie and Foster)
Shifted Magic — Altered Magic — Forged Magic
The Hidden Realm (Dawsyn and Cillian)
A Dragon's Wolf — A Dragon's Curse — A Dragon's Fate

Hopefully there will be plenty more series to come as the years continue, but for now, if you want to stay up to date on all the bookish things, or have any questions, join my reader group Heather Renee's Book Warriors on Facebook or send me an email anytime at HeatherReneeAuthor@yahoo.com.

I hope you enjoy this world as much as I have!

Also by Heather Renee

MYSTICS AND MAYHEM SERIES

The Hidden Realm

A new series within the Mystics and Mayhem world featuring wolf shifters and introducing dragon shifters! Releasing in 2023!

Fated to the Wolf

A complete New Adult Witch and Wolf series (dual POV) featuring an abandoned witch, a rogue wolf, and their broken bond.

Scorned by Blood

A complete New Adult Vampire series featuring a supernatural hunter and the sexy vampire bound to protect her no matter the cost.

Luna Marked

A complete New Adult wolf shifter series (dual POV) featuring a strong-willed leading lady and a patient, yet fierce alpha male.

Broken Court

A complete New Adult Urban Fantasy series featuring an unconventional and anti-heroine leading lady, a broody love interest, and a fae kingdom with a vile king.

INDIVIDUAL SERIES

Raven Point Pack Series

A complete Upper Young Adult Paranormal Romance series featuring wolves, witches, vengeance, and fated mates.

Shadow Veil Academy

A complete Upper Young Adult Urban Fantasy Academy series featuring shifters, elves, witches, and more.

Elite Supernatural Trackers

A complete New Adult Urban Fantasy series featuring witches, demons, a smart-mouthed female lead, alpha males, and a snarky fairy sidekick.

Royal Fae Guardians

A complete Young Adult Urban Fantasy series featuring fae, magic users, a sweet romance, along with snark and humor.

Blood of the Sea Series

A complete Young Adult Paranormal Romance series featuring vampires, open seas adventures, and the occasional pirate.

STANDALONE BOOKS

Ignite Me - A spicy wolf shifter story featuring a lost heir, the mate who doesn't want her, and the enemies who wish them dead.

Marked Paradox - A Young Adult fae story about a realm divided and one fae to bring them back together.

About the Author

Heather Renee is a USA Today Bestselling author who lives in Oregon. She writes Paranormal Romance and Urban Fantasy novels with a mixture of romance, humor, and sass. Her love of reading eventually led to her passion of writing and giving the gift of escapism.

When Heather's not writing, she's spending time with her loving husband and beautiful daughter, going on their own adventures. She loves to hear from her fans, so visit her website: www.HeatherReneeAuthor.com and check out the Contact Me page for ways to connect.

www.ingramcontent.com/pod-product-compliance
Lightning Source LLC
Chambersburg PA
CBHW061538210726
48287CB00006B/2002